My Sister Disappears

Lee Merrill Byrd

My Sister

Disappears

Stories and a Novella

Southern Methodist University Press

Dallas

These stories are works of fiction. Names, characters, places, and incidents are either the product of the author's imagination or are used fictitiously.

Requests for permission to reproduce material
from this work should be sent to:

Rights and Permissions
Southern Methodist University Press
Box 415
Dallas, Texas 75275

Some of the stories in this collection have appeared previously in the following publications: "Order and Disorder" in *North American Review* (1984) and *American Signatures, Nine New American Writers and Their Stories* (1986); "Hotter Here Than It Ever Was in New Jersey" in *Common Bonds: Stories by and about Modern Texas Women* (1990); and "Major Six Pockets" in *Blue Mesa Review* (1991).

Cover art: *Two Sisters* by Alfred Henry Maurer, c. 1923. Gouache on composition board, 21¾ × 18¼ in. Collection of the Modern Art Museum of Fort Worth. Gift of Mr. and Mrs. S. V. R. Spaulding, Jr.

Library of Congress Cataloging-in-Publication Data
Byrd, Lee Merrill.
My sister disappears : stories and a novella / Lee Merrill Byrd.—1st ed.
p.   cm.
ISBN 0-87074-351-1.
ISBN 0-87074-359-7 (pbk.)
I. Title.
PS3552.Y674M9   1993
813'.54—dc20   93-19647

To my mother

ALICE ROBINSON MERRILL

and to

SARAH LOUISE BAKER

October 21, 1974–December 26, 1992

. . .

FIGHTERS, REDHEADS BOTH

Contents

My Sister Disappears

Order and Disorder

There were three sets of clothes on Bunnie Gottis-man's bed. The set nearest the foot of the bed, neatly laid out, was for her husband, Ira. He would be wearing white linen slacks and a powder blue V-neck sweater of soft cashmere and, as though to insist that these were the clothes he would wear, Bunnie had smoothed them over and over again with her determined hand. In the V of the sweater she had put his gold necklace, the one that set his strong chest off to such advantage. She had formed a perfect circle with it and clasped it firmly shut. Below the carefully pressed slacks, she had laid a fresh pair of socks, side by side. A tin of brown shoe polish sat directly below the socks, on the floor, with a soft rag folded on top to remind her to shine Ira's shoes the minute he came home from the plant.

Next to Ira's clothes were the clothes that she would wear. At the very top, where her head would be if she were lying down, was a powder blue and white scarf to fix in her hair. She had tied it softly and made the ends even, exactly the way she would later when she put it on. Beside it were her earrings, tiny white pearls with gold posts. Right below the first scarf was a smaller one, all white, that she would place at her neck to accent the V of the cashmere sweater that was just like Ira's and, like Ira's, it was encircled with jewelry. But Bunnie had several necklaces—each one a different length—to draw the eye toward her breasts, which were still firm and youthful. She would be wearing white linen slacks, too. Below them, on the floor next to Ira's tin of shoe polish, she had placed her shoes, open-toed high heels of the same powder blue as her sweater.

The last set of clothes was folded in a pile at the top of the bed. These were for her son, Barry: a three-piece suit of a blue a shade darker than their sweaters; a white man-tailored shirt; a pair of white shoes with white socks edged in blue.

She would have to make a decision. Barry would need a warm jacket as soon as it got dark. There was the new one with the hood that her mother had just sent but that jacket was red and did not match. There was a second, a blue pea jacket that had been Ira's when he was a baby. Bunnie had had it dry-cleaned a month ago in anticipation of the party, but when she put it down on the bed between her outfit and Ira's she found the color too somber. The coat was too heavy. It was depressing. It reminded her of winter and she hated winter. Since the red did not match and the blue was depressing, they would leave before it got dark, no matter what Ira said.

It was two and Ira would be home by four to take them. Bunnie sat down on the edge of the bed, careful not to sit on any of the clothes she had laid out so neatly. Downstairs in the kitchen she could hear the maid cleaning up after lunch.

She leaned forward to look out the bedroom window into the back yard. There was Stephanie down below, sitting primly on the swing in her blue ruffled party dress. Her hair

810

00980900000010008001008010100

was braided and the braids were looped and tied with blue and white ribbons.

The leaves on the vines and on the trees were turning red. Some had fallen, staining the trim green lawn. Stephanie had picked up a leaf and was talking to it. Bunnie watched the serious turn of her face and the little mouth moving up and down.

Summer is over, said Bunnie out loud. She stood up close to the window for a long time, looking at Stephanie framed in the colors of autumn, and then she turned and inspected the pile of clothes for Barry and sat down again and re-arranged them so that the white shirt was tucked inside the vest and the vest was inside the suit jacket and the shoes, with the socks in them, sat right below the pants.

There, she said, you look very nice. She tugged at the sleeves of the jacket to make them straight. See how nice you look, she said.

She took a bath and sat on the edge of her bed wrapped in a towel while she put electric rollers in her hair. She could hear Stephanie's footsteps on the stairs. She was talking to herself.

No, I can't come outside, not now, not when I am ready for the party, Stephanie told the friend of her imagination. Bows in my hair, clean socks, ruffles, we are going to Amy's party—her voice rose—and you can't come.

Mommy? Stephanie stood at the door.

What, Stephie?

Is it time for the party yet?

No. Bunnie looked at the clock. Just a little bit more and Daddy will be home to take us. Where is your present? Show me where your present is.

Stephanie went back down the stairs, step-step on each step, her hand squeaking on the banister.

And don't get dirty.

Bunnie's hair was ash blonde, long and thick. She combed it out. The curl had taken just right, the waves over her temples were neither too tight nor too loose, the back had just enough body for a ponytail, her trademark since high school. She pivoted slowly to look at it in the mirror; it was exactly the way she liked it.

She leaned forward to study her face. Of all the women who would be at the party today, Bunnie was the only one who cared about the way she looked. She was always being mistaken for a teenager while her old friends looked old. Rivie Schwartz was even getting gray hair—and she didn't do a thing about it.

Rivie, said Bunnie, addressing the orderly row of cosmetic bottles on her bureau, it's no crime to keep yourself up, you know. You could lose ten, even twenty pounds and put some color on your hair and you'd be gorgeous. What was the use? Rivie Schwartz never listened. Rivie had a theory and her theory was that as long as you were happy it didn't matter what you looked like.

She turned away from the bureau and got the blue and white scarf off the bed, wrapping it around the ponytail so that the ends of the scarf were perfectly balanced. With a tiny brush, she applied a rich coral-colored lipstick, taking pains to follow the exact shape of her mouth. She stood back and looked at herself. She looked good.

The clock on the dresser said a quarter to three. Bunnie unwrapped the towel and put on a pair of baby blue bikini underpants and a matching bra that held her very high. With a robe to cover herself until she got dressed, she sat down again on the edge of the bed and lit a cigarette. She had to talk to Ira. She dialed the plant.

Ira? It's me. Listen, come home a little early, will you, so you can take a bath.

Ira's secretary was in his office, asking him a question.

Tell them to do it now, Bunnie heard him tell the girl. He sounded tired.

Ira? said Bunnie.

I took a bath this morning, he snapped into the phone.

That was hours ago, Ira. You know how you sweat. Listen. Are you there? Ira? There was muffled conversation between him and the secretary. Ira? Can't you talk to her later?

Yeah. Yeah. Go ahead.

Listen. I'm going to lay out your blue sweater, the one with the V-neck. And what pants? Your white slacks?

Come on, Bunnie. It's just a picnic. Something casual.

Your white slacks *are* casual, Ira.

Some jeans. There's a pair in my closet back from the cleaners.

Ira. You look much better in those slacks.

The guys'll be playing ball, for godsakes.

Ira?

What?

I have your white slacks laid out already. With the blue sweater. It took me two hours to decide.

Bunnie . . .

We were going to look real nice, she said quickly.

Listen. She heard him tapping his fingers on the top of his desk. Everyone there is going to be wearing jeans. Okay? Have you ever seen Rivie Schwartz in anything but jeans? And Fay . . . Fay and Becky'll be wearing jeans and all the kids'll have on whatever. It's just a picnic, Bunnie.

He had his hand over the phone again, talking to the girl.

Ira? Ira? said Bunnie frantically. Stephanie has on her blue party dress, the one with the ruffles with the white pinafore and the white tights. Ira?

Yeah. Okay, she heard him say to the secretary.

She looks real cute, Ira. Her hair's in braids with blue ribbons.

He was back on the line. You dress her up too much, Bunnie, he said flatly. She won't have any fun. Put on the little shorts and the top your mother sent and some sneakers.

I can't do that. I spent all morning getting her ready.

So what?

No, that's what!

Now don't go getting upset, Bunnie.

I'm not upset, Ira. Do you hear me? I'm not upset. We just won't look good. If Rivie Schwartz wants to look that way, let her. If she wants her kids running around looking like slobs, okay. But I'm not going to do that, Ira. I'm just not going to do that.

Okay. Okay. Bunnie? Listen. Don't cry. Come on now, don't cry.

The secretary was talking again. Later, he said to her sharply, I'm on the phone.

Bunnie? You okay?

Yeah.

Listen. What's Barry wearing?

He's sleeping.

He is? Maybe he'll still be sleeping. We'll leave him home. Tina can watch him.

Leave him home? What do you mean? What are you talking about?

Okay. Okay. Don't yell, Bunnie. I was just trying to help you out.

We said we weren't going to leave him home.

Yeah.

Remember?

Yeah. Well . . .

What?

Ask Tina will she come, too.

To the party?

Yeah. Why not?

You can't take a maid . . .

Yeah, you can. Yeah, you can. Let Tina carry him. He's too heavy for you. You won't have to be walking around carrying him the whole time.

She didn't answer.

Yeah, tell her. Tell her I'll pay her a little extra. She can have Saturday night off, too, if she wants it. Then you can sit around and talk to the girls the way you've been wanting to. You haven't been out in a long time.

Bunnie put her hand out and touched the blue suit she had fixed for Barry. She stared at the polished shoes.

Listen, baby, Ira said. I've got to get off. I got some stuff I have to do before I leave. He hung up.

Stephanie was back with the present.

Why are you crying, Mommy?

Come here, said Bunnie, holding her arms out for Stephanie. She picked her up and put her down next to Barry's suit and then she sat down on her knees beside the bed with her arms still around Stephanie.

It makes me sick, she said. See how beautiful you are. See how beautiful you look—the little ruffles, the blue dress.

Don't cry, Mommy.

I have to. I have to cry. It makes me feel so sick. God, what will I do? She got up and carried Stephanie into the nursery. Barry lay in his crib, still sleeping.

Daddy says to wear shorts and sneakers, whispered Bunnie. Is that what you want to wear, shorts and sneakers?

Shorts and sneakers?

He says, Wear shorts and sneakers, and Barry should come with Tina.

Tina?

So I can sit and talk to the girls, he says.

She put Stephanie in a little red chair in a corner of the nursery, and then she knelt down and began to unbuckle her party shoes. Stephanie pinched her lips together and squinted at her mother.

Mommy? Is Barry one years old yet?

No.

Is Mona?

No.

How old is Mona?

Six months.

Is Barry six months?

No, Barry is nine months. Let me have your other foot . . . and Stephie?

What?

Let's not talk right now, okay, sweetheart? I got a headache.

Okay. Mommy? Mona can sit up.

Yeah. Okay.

She's a nice little baby. You know what she does, Mommy?

Stephie . . .

When you hold her, she licks your face. She pulls your hair.

Stephanie!

Bunnie pushed Stephanie's legs away from her. She stood up and tried to look through Stephanie's bureau for her shorts but her eyes were full of tears and she felt so tired suddenly that she left the nursery and went back into her room. She pulled the bedspread off so that the clothes, which had been as orderly as soldiers, fell to the floor in confusion. She got in underneath the covers and tried to get warm.

Stephanie came into the room, red-faced and miserable, and stood next to the bed.

Mommy? The clothes are all over the floor.

It doesn't matter anymore, Bunnie said.

Mommy? What will I wear?

What do you want to wear?

I don't know. Can't you help me?

No. I'm going to sleep for a while.

Stephanie crawled up next to her mother. Bunnie curled around her and shivered. She shut her eyes and tried to rest, but couldn't. She rolled over and stared out the back windows. From where she lay she could see the tops of the old oak trees in whose patriarchal shadows they had imagined the seasons of their lives would pass. It was for those watchful trees and the sloping yard they shaded that Bunnie and Ira Gottisman had bought this old house.

Bunnie remembered the day they had first stood at these windows. She was pregnant then, with Barry. Ira held Stephanie in his arms, so she could look out the windows at the trees and the yard.

All the children of all our friends will come and play in our back yard, Bunnie remembered herself saying. Because it's so big and because these trees will make it dark and cool, even on the hottest days of summer. The three of them stared down, imagining. We'll have birthday parties and wienie roasts and picnics . . . and a sandbox—right underneath the trees—with a wading pool and a swing set beside it.

And we'll play baseball, Ira had interjected solemnly. All the fathers and all the sons.

Yes, Bunnie remembered she had agreed, her voice as serious as his.

Because it wasn't going to be anything but a boy, Bunnie said out loud, addressing the huge trees. One girl and one boy. A perfectly matched set.

Bunnie Gottisman heard the car pull in the driveway. She frowned at the clock. Three-twenty.

Here comes your father, she said. She held herself tight, imagining the front door opening. Ira would bustle inside. Why aren't you ready? he'd say. Come on, come on, what's your problem? She shut her eyes.

He slammed the front door shut. I'm home, honey!

Here we are, Daddy! called Stephanie, sitting up in bed.

9

Bunnie heard him take the steps, two at a time. He stood at the bedroom door. Bunnie? What's the matter? Why aren't you ready?

Are we going to the party, Daddy? asked Stephanie, bouncing up and down on the bed.

Of course we're going to the party. Now give Daddy a kiss and run down and tell Tina to get ready to go. Hurry.

Ira came around the bed to where he could see Bunnie's face. What are you doing? he asked her.

I'm asleep, she said.

What do you mean, you're asleep?

I'm asleep.

What about the party?

I'm not going to the party.

What do you mean, you're not going to the party? You've been talking about nothing else but this party for months.

I mentioned it twice, Ira.

Twice! You said, Amy's birthday, Amy's birthday ever since Barry was born. When Rivie has Amy's birthday in September, I'll go out, you said. Remember what you said, Bunnie?

But now I'm not going. I'm not going to go to any party wearing jeans.

Is that what it is? Now you're going to blame it on me, because I want to wear jeans, huh?

And Stephanie in shorts and sneakers. I can't do it, Ira.

He sat down in a chair next to the bed. Bunnie, get this through your head. It's just a picnic, see. It's a picnic for Amy's birthday. It's all our friends. Friends we've known all our lives. It's at the park, Greenbrook Park, where we used to play when we were kids. Remember, Bunnie? Come on, did you ever go to Greenbrook Park in a ruffled dress?

My mother always got us dressed up, Ira. I always wore a ruffled dress and my mother always wore her . . . white linen slacks and her blue cashmere sweater and my father wore his to match. And they looked very nice, Ira Gottisman. Don't you remember how nice my mother and father always looked? And everyone always said, Look at the Farbers. Aren't the Farbers a perfectly beautiful family?

Bunnie . . .

That's the way it always was, Ira.

You've been in the house too long, Bunnie.

She started to cry. He leaned over and touched her hair.

We have to go, he said.

You go, Ira. You go and take Stephanie, put her in her shorts and sneakers and you wear your jeans. Everybody will be real glad to see you.

They want to see you, Bunnie. Everybody loves you.

Well, I don't love them. I don't want to see any of them or any of their goddamn kids, do you hear me, Ira?

Yeah. Her shouting frightened him. He sat without knowing what to do while Bunnie turned away from him and cried. He relaxed in the chair, studying his hands, nearly falling asleep, waiting. When he opened his eyes, she had turned back and was looking at him. Ira? she said. It's too much.

No, it's not, Bunnie. He leaned forward and smoothed her hair away from her forehead. It's going to be fine, sweetheart. Everyone will be so glad to see us. We're going to look good—I promise—the way we always do. You always look good, Bunnie, no matter what you wear, you always look so good. Everyone will say, Look how good that Ira Gottisman looks in his jeans and his blue sweater. And who's that woman he's with? Bunnie smiled at him. My God! It's Bunnie Gottisman! And would you look at those incredible jeans she's wearing! That made Bunnie laugh. And see there, there's little Stephanie Gottisman in her sparkling shorts and sneakers . . .

But he had lost her. She was looking past him, out the

window to the yard and the old oak trees and she was crying again. He leaned back in his chair and looked at the floor.

Everyone will want to tell us, Ira.

No, they won't, Bunnie.

Yeah, they will. I know a doctor here, there's a doctor here. There's a home in Hackensack for kids like that. She put her hands over her face. Rivie Schwartz will say, That's a nice home up there in Hackensack, it's not like you've heard of with the long dull lonely rooms where they live for a thousand years strapped in iron beds shitting all over themselves, oh, it's real pretty, Bunnie . . .

Shut up, Bunnie.

They'll have all kinds of advice, Ira. Everyone will want to tell us.

You're dreaming, Bunnie.

I'm dreaming?!

He grabbed her arm. It's just his eyes, right? You tell them we've been to the doctor's, bunch of doctors, they say it's just his eyes, when they fix his eyes he's gonna be just like everyone else. College, a good job, marriage, the works . . .

Come off it, Ira.

There's nothing wrong with him!

Don't yell at me, Ira. Come on, don't you yell at me. Where are you all day, for godsakes?

Where am I? Where am I? What do you mean, where am I? I'm down at that goddamn plant seven days a week trying to keep it from falling apart. Where the hell you want me to be?

She sat up, throwing the bedclothes off her legs. I want you to be home, Ira. If you were home, you wouldn't say that.

Ira got up out of the chair and turned away from her, toward the back windows.

Nine months old and he can't even hold his head up, she said.

She watched his back as he stared out over their yard.

There's something wrong with him, Ira, she said. There is. It's not just his eyes, no matter what those doctors say. She kicked at one of the blue cashmere sweaters that lay on the floor. There's something so wrong with him.

Bunnie got up off the bed and went to her closet. She pushed aside some dresses and felt for her pants. There was a black pair of jeans. She pulled them off the hanger and put them on. In the back of her closet were shelves where she kept clothes that she intended to give away, and she grabbed a cotton jersey from there and jerked it over her head. It fell to her hips like a sack, in black and brown stripes. She stood in front of the mirror looking at herself, watching what she could of Ira's trembling back, and the tears ran all down her face.

There, she said. Do you think Rivie Schwartz will like that? Do you think I look hopeless enough to be the mother of . . .

But he was behind her already, holding her, and she couldn't stop crying.

Oh, my God, she said, over and over again, what will we ever do?

Sssssh, sssssh, he whispered. Don't cry. He took her away from the mirror, over to the bed, and he made her sit down.

Don't cry, he said again. She watched his shoes as he stood, inert and helpless, in front of her, the way he always stood when he didn't know what to do. After a while, he walked away. She heard him on the other side of the bed. He had picked up all the clothes that she had laid out so carefully for the picnic and brought them back beside her. He spread them out again for her to see.

Was it like this? he asked her, smoothing the clothes the way he knew she would have done. She nodded solemnly.

Here, he said. He cleared his throat. Lift your arms up. He pulled the shapeless jersey over her head. He took the cashmere sweater and he put it on her, tugging it slightly at the waist. He held out the white linen slacks and he made her take the jeans off and put the white slacks on. He slipped on her shoes, the open-toed high heels of powder blue, and then he found the necklaces she had set out and he put them on her, one by one, adjusting them so that they would look just the way he knew she liked them to look, and then he put in her earrings—the white pearls—his broad, trembling fingers awkward with the gold posts.

Come here, he said, and he led her over to her bureau and combed her long, thick hair and straightened the ends of her scarf so that they were perfectly balanced and powdered her face carefully so that no one would know.

There, he said. See how pretty you are. See how beautiful.

Major Six Pockets

Tennessee sprang out the car door the minute John turned the handle, barking across the low rainy meadow at the four steaming cows; they lumbered down towards the stream, their leader—the biggest one—turning suddenly, clumsily, pawing the ground.

Daddy! shrieked Andy. They're going to kill Tennessee. But no, said Daddy, it was not true. That cow who pawed the ground was a woman, Daddy said—can't you see her tits hanging down?—and women cows are hopeless in the face of a dog like Tennessee.

Now, if that was a bull, said Daddy, raising his eyebrows. Um um um . . .

Yes, said Andy, raising what little eyebrows remained to him, if that was a bull. Um um um . . .

John hung out the car door, marking the landscape like a tour guide, while Daddy bumped the Mazda down into place beside a pile of branches. Here, said John, is the firewood. And here is a bush. Yes, here is where we park. There is the water.

Daddy said, Here it is, the perfect camping spot. Just like I told you from the beginning. We got out of the car and stood looking up at the soft gray clouds that huddled at the mouth of the canyon. Susie got out and stood beside Daddy, and John and Andy came and fell in place. They looked things over, the indolent sky, the steep mountains, the flat meadow skirted with chokecherry bushes, the pile of branches, the white rocks already set for a campfire. Up above, a long distance off, a last lone car rumbled on through the San Juans.

Here it is, said Andy. The perfect camping spot.

Here is where it began, with Tennessee and the imitation bull and with the finding of this spot, the perfect camping spot, as Daddy called it. Here is where it began, the vacating, the vacation, here on the low secret meadow, hidden in a pocket of the ragged mountains.

But it had started for Daddy a long time before that, the talking about it, the working out of it. It had started for Daddy almost from the beginning, before we knew about Andy, which way he would go, before he lost the ear and his hair and then the fingers on his left hand; long before it became apparent about John and his face. It had started for Daddy almost from the beginning, when Andy lay on a high bed, in isolation, wrapped in white gauze, and did not talk. Daddy would talk to him, would talk to him about it, about the trip we would take, about the vacation, about the mountains and the perfect camping spot. Daddy said they would catch fish, they would catch rainbow trout, they would catch browns and cutthroats, they would use flies and worms and salmon eggs, garlic-flavored marshmallows and grasshoppers, and they would take the fish and Mother would cook them over the campfire in a pan filled with butter. Daddy said they would ask Susie to fry potatoes, too, and there would be Cokes and Jewish pickles and later some dessert.

One day in March after a long night and a high fever, Andy in a thin and broken whisper said he wanted pie. Cherry pie. The nurse said they didn't have any. Daddy's voice began to shake. He told her it didn't matter, that Andy didn't want the cherry pie now, he wanted the cherry pie for later, for after the fish. Wasn't that right? Daddy asked Andy and Andy shut his eyes and nodded solemnly.

Daddy, when he went to visit John on the ward, told John all about the plans he and Andy had been making. Daddy said he'd talked to Andy about where Eskimos lived, and that Andy seemed to agree that that might be the perfect place for a camping trip. Did John know that there in that place where Eskimos lived everyone slept together naked under a mound of caribou furs and there were lots of girls and all the girls liked to dance?

John listened intently, chewing on the bandages that covered his hands. He did not think that he wanted to camp in a place like that. He would rather camp in a place that was just so-so where if there were any girls they didn't dance and if you slept under caribou furs you could wear your pajamas.

Daddy talked to Ronnie Tate in the bed next to John's and wondered what kind of son he had who did not like girls who danced. He asked Carnell Hughes on the other side of the room what he thought about sleeping naked and the three young boys giggled and waited for Daddy to come back. When he did he sat on a chair in the middle of the room and brought news of Andy and the latest plans.

On the first of April, they took Andy out of isolation and put him in the big room with John and with Ronnie Tate and with Carnell Hughes. Andy looked at John and said, His skin, and John said in his most matter-of-fact way, He's bald. Daddy laughed until he cried and began to sing, Christmas is a-coming, the geese are getting fat, and clapped his hands until John wailed, Oh Daddy, stop.

That same day after lunch Daddy went to Colonel Bubbie's Army-Navy Surplus and bought a pair of shorts, Italian six-pockets, and filled the pockets with stuff for the trip: a pocket knife, some fish hooks and salmon eggs, fishing line and candy bars, and they spent the afternoon eating Milky Ways and looking over Daddy's Italian six-pockets and talking about Alaska and the Ozarks and New Mexico, about the Rockies and the Blue Hills and other perfect camping spots.

But April was no better. Andy's blood was full of infection. The antibiotic they gave him to cure it made him throw up and he could not talk. The tub men came to get him in the mornings, to scrub the dead skin away from the burns, and Andy screamed and Daddy walked the halls. He wasn't sure where we would go anymore and he agreed with John, that a so-so place would be just as good as a place where Eskimos lived.

The doctors said they needed to operate on Andy again and that John had a staph infection in the graft on his cheek and must have more IVs. Ronnie Tate said would Daddy tell them again about the Eskimos and the dancing girls but Daddy said he'd have to wait, he did not want to talk about the trip anymore for a little while.

In the evening two days after Andy's surgery, Daddy and the nurse lifted Andy onto a chair and the nurse said that Andy would have to sit there awhile for a change and Andy cried and cried and said he hurt and the nurse finally asked Daddy to step out in the hall. Later, Daddy and the nurse put Andy back in bed, one under his head, one holding his feet, there being no place in between that they could touch, and they covered him with a sheet and tucked it in and Andy began to talk and did not stop. He said to John that he was sorry about John's corduroy coat, that he had worn John's corduroy coat that day and that it had gotten burned and did Daddy know where the corduroy coat was or his blue pants, the ones he had worn while they played in the fort and had he lost his sneakers too, the new ones, and did John remember how Morgan had thrown dirt on him to make the fire go out and did John remember the ice cream man who called the fire engine and did Mom know how to cook fish and that after the fish they would have cherry pie. He shook all over, he talked so fast and he said that he liked the Italian six-pockets and he called Daddy Major Six Pockets and Daddy sat down and could not talk.

Then the plans began in earnest. And every day they discussed another place. There were the Chiricahuas and the Sangre de Cristos, the Smokies in Tennessee where Daddy was born, the Mississippi and the Shenandoah. There was Missoula and Butte and Chaco Canyon and Mesa Verde and Cheyenne and the Florida Keys and the Yucatan and the Black Hills.

But—much later, when the boys were home again—Susie said she just wanted to go to Colorado, because, after all, that was where she was born; and according to the things that she had heard about Colorado from Daddy, there was a cottage there in a big meadow, a little honeymoon cottage where she had once lived and surrounding that cottage were hills and mountains where elk and deer roamed, snakes and mountain lions and coyotes. And in the meadow bulls moaned and pranced and down around all of it came crashing the mighty Rio Grande. She was a true Colorado girl and needed to go back. As proof, she reminded the boys that when she was hardly a day old, she had played naked in ten or more feet of snow. Hadn't Daddy said so?

And so the vacation was to Colorado, to Susie's ancestral homeland because, Daddy said, Susie is the oldest and even though we won't get to go where the boys wanted to go, all the things that they had dreamed about and talked about while they were in the hospital were right there in Colorado:

cherry pies and caribou furs and dancing girls and sleeping bags and perfect camping spots. And anyway, Daddy said, it would have to be Susie's trip because the fire had been the boys'.

Andy took Dr. Phineas, the green frog, and Smudge, the stuffed bear. Also, he needed a backpack. He filled its pockets and corners with erasers and magnets, some photos he had gotten from Grandma, pennies, crayons, and a ruler. Dr. Phineas nearly fell out, even with Smudge crammed in beside him, so it seemed necessary to bring a second brown bear to make the fit complete.

John had books, many more than one, because of Andy and all the things that Andy had in his backpack. And John brought tapes and what were tapes without the tape recorder?

Daddy helped Susie hide her violin between the cooler and the back seat beneath two sleeping bags. She put a shoe box containing her diaries and some pesos and soap and a small tea set and a something she was crocheting under the front seat and stuffed her jacket in behind it.

Daddy brought books and a pad of paper to write on in case of a poem. There was mayonnaise and peanut butter and salami and crackers and instant coffee, plenty of bacon, sacks of oranges and apples, a pineapple from Mexico, and some sugarless chewing gum. There was a hatchet and a shovel and two delicate fishing rods jammed in between the seats and the doors. The trunk strapped to the roof held a change of clothes for every person for every eventuality, but for the most part, it was full of pressure garments for the boys and splints and ace wraps and gauze and adhesive tape.

Well, said Daddy. None of this takes up much room.

*   *   *

Susie sat in the front seat and talked. She said that Texas was all right. Though it was hot. Though of course El Paso was not as hot as the rest of Texas. El Paso was not really at all like any other part of Texas. In the first place there were no Texans in El Paso. In the second place there was Juarez and all of that. Daddy listened and dreamed and Susie talked intently. John snoozed, his left eye partly open even while he slept, and Andy colored, Dr. Phineas looking on. Tennessee turned and sighed between the cooler and the violin and the five extra pairs of shoes.

Daddy drove on up through Hatch and Truth or Consequences, on past Albuquerque and Santa Fe and Española, all in one day, driving towards Colorado and the perfect camping spot. Why did you and Mom ever leave Colorado in the first place? asked Susie. I mean, if you worked for Texas millionaires and ate venison and had the honeymoon cottage all to yourselves and the Rio Grande in your back yard?

John and Andy leaned forward to listen. Your mother and I, said Daddy, had things to do.

Yeah? said Susie. Like what?

Your mother and I had work cut out for us in the big city. We couldn't work for Texas millionaires forever. It was too easy.

Anyway, he went on, we were warned in a dream that John would arrive any minute and that he intended to be born in Albuquerque, in a little rent house in Albuquerque where the landlord next door was always drunk, so we had to quick hustle and pack up and move down the Rio Grande.

Oh, Daddy . . .

Tres Piedras had a cafe and a grocery and two gas stations.

Well, said Daddy, there was a second dream. It said, Leave any minute for Las Cruces for Andy intends to come howling and screaming forth from his mother's belly at exactly five in the morning on the twenty-fifth day . . .

Andy sang to himself all across the high plain between Tres Piedras and Antonito, hanging his good arm out the window.

John peered into the tape recorder listening to the Lone Ranger talk things over with Tonto. The Cavendish gang had just killed the Lone Ranger's brother and all his friends. Those evil men knew the Lone Ranger by sight. If they know that one man escaped their ambush, worried the Lone Ranger, they'll look for him and kill him.

Them not know one man escape, said Tonto. Tonto bury five men, make six graves. Crook think you die with others.

Good, wheezed the Lone Ranger. Then my name shall be buried forever with my brother and my friends. From now on my face must be concealed. A disguise, perhaps, he considered. Or maybe a mask. That's it! A mask . . .

Daddy wore his Italian six-pockets: two pockets on the side, two pockets in the front, two pockets behind, with four buttons up the fly that he never managed to button all at once. John and Andy wore their masks, brown elastic hoods that held white life masks in place. Susie wore a straw hat and people stared. Daddy stopped in Albuquerque for gas and people stared. We stopped in Ojo Caliente for lunch and took the boys' masks off so they could eat and everyone in the restaurant grew quiet and tried to pretend they didn't notice. In Antonito we stopped to buy flies and hooks and everybody watched while Daddy discussed salmon eggs loudly and deliberately with his children, Andy breathing hard and fast from the pressure of the mask on his nose, John, solemn and intent, just his eyes, his lips.

From Antonito on, Daddy drove hard, pushing on into the mountains, looking for that conjunction of the perfect camping spot and the setting sun.

*   *   *

The road from Antonito towards Platoro was all dirt and rocks and Daddy drove it fast, the Mazda eclipsed by the rising dust. Tennessee stood up, his nose pressed against the window, swaying as Daddy took the curves. Susie said how late it was, and John said that Daddy drove too fast. After a few miles there was a sign, a tent pitched upon solid rock, and behind the sign among the trees a neat circle of cars and RVs just settling down for some outdoor adventure and Susie said, There it is, Daddy, there's the perfect camping spot, but Daddy only drove faster, on past more signs with pitched tents, drawing up toward the edge of the wrong side of the road from time to time to peer down through thick forest, over sheer cliffs. We're getting closer, he said, as eager as Tennessee.

The forest opened up into meadow that rolled away from the road toward the hills. Daddy slowed to look, sticking his head out the window, talking it over. There's a stream. Too close to the road. What do you think?

But nothing seemed quite right and Daddy drove on.

There is no perfect camping spot, said Susie. It will be dark and we'll be lost and it will be cold and it will rain.

Daddy turned off the road, to the left, down a rutted path that crossed a little bridge and went up on top of a hill. Let's look around, he said.

Andy and John and Daddy got out and stood looking through the trees at the flat green meadow below. They walked down some and the three of them peed while Susie sat in the front seat and watched until they disappeared and watched the same spot until they came back again. They got in the car.

Well, Sus, said Daddy, I think we've found it.

The road down from the hill to the perfect camping spot was pitted with animal holes and big hidden rocks and at one point was so slanted that the Mazda felt as if it would tip over. The last curve revealed the meadow, empty and waiting.

The sun began its long summer descent at one end of the slender canyon while the ragged clouds pushed for entrance at the other; down in between, in the long flat meadow, our camp took its shape: tent and Mazda, firewood, cooler, trunk, sleeping bags. Daddy built a fire for the supper and said he thought he might try to fish while he waited for the fire to make coals. The kids each declared that they would go first, until Daddy said that for tonight, since it was almost dark, he was the only one who could fish. But that they could watch. And if they were good maybe they could each hold the pole once. Maybe twice. And that though they would bring the second pole, they probably wouldn't use it since fly fishing was an art that had to be taught and it was getting too dark to do any teaching.

They walked up the meadow, carrying the two poles, looking for a pool of water in the stream where trouts and browns and cutthroats would be congregating. Tennessee made wide circles around them, Daddy in his six-pockets and sneakers, Susie in her straw hat, the boys masked and splinted. Just as the sun hit the edge of the mountain, they were back, unmasked and unsplinted, shoes and shorts and six-pockets soaking. Daddy said here was proof that every camping trip required an extra set of shoes and they all changed and stood around the campfire while Daddy told them again about his backpacking trip through the Waminuches with Uncle Steve and how Uncle Steve and he had been caught in a driving rain and had to quick set up their tent and how he had had to rub Uncle Steve's hands and feet because Uncle Steve was shaking so hard from the cold. But how that was the price a person had to pay when he went camping with skinny people.

After supper Daddy said, Let's get up early and go fishing first thing. The kids got into the tent and laughed and argued for a long time, about whose head should be where, and about who would have Tennessee sleeping next to him, and about how loud John snored with his mask on. Daddy roamed around the campfire, getting things ready for the morning, looking up at the sky from time to time. He had a cigarette and some tequila and sat on a log, staring into the fire, listening to the kids talk. Much later, when they had finally fallen asleep, he covered the coals with dirt and made a bed on the ground near the door of the tent, but the minute he got in his bag it started to rain, so he came up into the Mazda, where the back seat was pulled down.

Think you're smart, do you? he said, making room for himself. We slept the way you sleep the first night on camping trips, just so-so, sometimes resting so deep inside the sound of the rain, sometimes sore, turning and turning to find just the right position. Then just before dawn, he woke up suddenly and said, I think the kids are having fun, don't you? and went back to sleep as if that was that: the very last thing on his mind.

That first morning he taught them to fish. They went back to the deep pool up the meadow before breakfast. He showed them how to cast, how to let the attractive, glittering flies float along the water as if they were alive, how to turn the reel quickly and strike again to catch the attention of those trouts and browns and cutthroats who lay waiting fat and sleek to take the bait. The flies caught on every rock and bush and Andy when they came back described the way in which Major Six Pockets had waded in and out of the deep pool to recover the line and how they hadn't caught anything this time because Tennessee had been leaping up and down the stream and barking after cows and scaring the fish and how

Susie and John had taken much more than their share of turns. When Susie wasn't listening, Daddy said she fly fished as if she'd been casting in the womb.

For breakfast there were eggs cooked in plenty of bacon grease, the sun coming up sly and warm along the mouth of the canyon. Afterward, Daddy boiled water over the fire and took it and Andy to the stream to bathe. From a distance Andy looked like he wore a coat of armor across his chest and back, the skin was so scarred there and still so furious and red and it drew down tight against the soft whiteness of his stomach. Daddy washed him all over with warm water and then made him lie down quick to rinse off. He said how Andy was the only boy he knew who had only seven fingers but ten belly buttons and together they traced the convolutions that erupted on the upper part of his body. Andy said that John and Susie had to take a bath too but Daddy said no, that Susie being not burned could bathe every three or four days the way you did on camping trips and that John having no more open spots on his body could wait until tomorrow. Andy fussed and cried and said it was not fair, that just because he was burned he had to bathe every day. Daddy carried him to the Mazda and laid him down so he could pick the dead skin away from the open spots. Andy studied the slow movement of the sterile tweezers in Daddy's hand while Daddy strained and squinted to avoid the raw skin and Andy's screams, and rubbed cream on him, ranging slowly and methodically over that small eroded chest with his fingertips, massaging the withered arm with his whole hand, and wrapped both with ace wraps and put the pressure garments and the splints and the mask back on. Tennessee licked the bacon grease out of the fry pan and Daddy said that he would like to try fishing on the other part of the stream. Susie and John grabbed the poles. Let your mother go first, said Daddy. Susie came next, pressing close, then John, then Daddy and Andy with Tennessee behind and in front and behind again, announcing himself to the trout and browns and cutthroats who waited fat and sleek in the deep pools at the top of the meadow.

The stream crossed the meadow east not a hundred yards from the perfect camping spot. There was a little trail there on the other side but Andy said he could not walk, that his shoes were so wet from walking across the stream with them on and that Daddy would have to carry him. He cried and fell down in a heap insisting that he could not keep going, that his squeaking shoes hurt his feet, and Daddy stopped, not sure whether to go on or to go back. Susie said that Andrew was a baby and John said that it was nothing to walk in wet shoes and Andy wailed. We walked on ahead, Susie and John looking back every little bit to watch Daddy kneeling beside Andy, taking his shoes and socks off and squeezing the water out; they could see Daddy talking to Andy and trying to shut him up. Susie called back for them to hurry up and Daddy told her just to go on and mind her own business. Susie yelled to Andy that her shoes were already dry and Daddy said to shut up, just shut up, so we went on, up where the chokecherries got thicker and the trees were taller and the sun not quite so bright to hurt the boys' skin.

After a while Daddy came up with Andy behind him sulking. One of the fishing lines was all tangled up and Daddy sat cross-legged on the ground trying to straighten it while Susie demonstrated the art of casting to her brothers. She stood on a big rock and repeated all of Daddy's instructions on fly fishing as if they were her own and John and Andy watched her, caught by the volume of what she knew, mesmerized by each toss into the glimmering pool. Daddy looked up and looking, was arrested by the sight of the children: Susie, high on the rock, in her eleventh year suddenly so tall and beautiful; John, his face turned up to listen to her, that face that no amount of studying could change, the one side ravaged by fire, the other side handsome, perfect; Andy, at the age of six, bald, without an ear, with only seven fingers. Daddy looked. They played, mindless of him, mindless of themselves, laughing. And the line lay tangled across his knees.

We fished there an hour, then walked on up the canyon, up a trail toward the steep mountains, climbing until Andy's complaints were unbearable, and then found a place to sit while Daddy took out the map. He traced the road between Antonito and Platoro with his finger and located the perfect camping spot somewhere in between. Susie said if we drove farther up we would find Blowout Pass and Cornwall's Nose and John said, Look, here is Elephant Mountain and Handkerchief Mesa and Andy because he could not read screamed until he could squeeze in close to Daddy and touch the map himself. Daddy took Andy's finger and led it all over the local terrain until it fell with a thud into Lost Lake.

Then Daddy lit a cigarette and pointed to the mountains in front of him, mountains that erupted from the earth, pocked with sinuous ridges and red the color of dirt, and said those were called the Pinnacles and John wanted to know why and how come they were the way they were. Daddy looked at John awhile and didn't answer, as if he hadn't heard, so John asked again and Daddy said abruptly they were called the Pinnacles because they went straight up and were like towers and that the Pinnacles and all the mountains around, the whole range of the San Juans, were formed by fire.

They fished all that afternoon, before and after supper, but it wasn't until the next day, until they began to act as if they'd been in that canyon all their lives, that anything was caught.

It was just before supper and they had gone again to that deep pool where they had gone the first time; and John came back across the meadow alone, his hands behind him and grinning, with the fish and the story. It was Susie's fish, he said, and her line had been so tight and she screamed, Daddy, it's a fish, but Daddy had gotten mad and said he was tired of wading out into the pool to untangle their lines and that people were going to either have to learn to cast or learn to wade. Susie screamed and screamed and Andy and John screamed and screamed, trying to persuade Daddy that this was no false alarm, but Daddy said it was a rock and that this was the last time, that in nothing less than two days he had nearly ruined his sneakers.

John said, Daddy waded out and put his hand down to get the line and when he brought it up, there it was, the fish, and Daddy laughed and slapped the water and Susie said, See Daddy. See Daddy, and Daddy sent John back to spread the news. Come on, Mom, he said and we walked back across the meadow to hear the story again, once from Daddy and once from Susie and once more from Andy. We stayed there by the pool until they could barely see, until two more fish were caught, and then came back to the perfect camping spot and ate them, cooked over the campfire in a pan filled with butter, each bite causing Daddy to tell the story again, until Susie's first catch had settled forever in the memories of the children, until just the smell of fish or the sight of the moon or the feel of mountain air on their bodies would remind them again all through their lives of their Daddy and the trip he took them on into the mountains that first year after the fire.

That night the kids went to bed early, right after they ate, because they wanted to get up first thing and catch another fish. Tennessee crawled in the tent beside them, exhausted.

Daddy wanted to talk. He sat beside the fire. He said he wondered did every parent think that only his own kids were remarkable? He smoothed a pattern into the dirt with his shoe, going over and over it until it was a perfect little fan shape, edged on both sides. Don't you think the kids are remarkable? he said. He could not believe how the fire had changed them all, he could not believe how happy they always were. It was what he would have wanted them to be, but never just by telling them could have made them that way. Do you see what I mean? he asked. It was like the fire itself had given them what we never could have.

He leaned forward, his elbows on his knees, and took a piece of his hair and twisted it around and around his finger, staring off to where the mountains lay like paper silhouettes against the sky. After a while he said, Don't you think John's face is getting better? Don't you think that eye is not pulling down quite so much?

They fished all that week, most often in the deep pool just down below the perfect camping spot, but sometimes up the meadow; once Daddy even got everybody in the car and went on up the road as if he were going to Platoro. He stopped at Saddle Creek, a wide stream that wound like a snake through a damp high grassed plain. It was flat there and the wind blew.

There was a man at Saddle Creek. He came walking up the stream wearing high rubber boots with his pole in his hand and his fish basket across his shoulder, walking slow, his eyes on the water. He was the first person we had seen since the vacation began and Daddy when he saw him got excited and said so quickly, Say, how's the fishing? The man looked up and blinked at Daddy and then past Daddy and past Susie at John and Andy and no further. Andy had his splint off and John wore his mask. The man stopped and blinked again;

and Daddy remembering moved back some and directly in front of Andy. How's the fishing? Daddy said again.

The man had been drinking. It was noon and he smelled like cheap wine. He didn't move. What do you have there? he said to Daddy. Daddy's face got tight. Behind your back? said the man. Daddy said, It's my family. The man opened his mouth so slow and looked as if he was going to fall forward; he sneezed suddenly and took an old handkerchief out of his pocket to wipe his nose.

Yeah? he said. He stared at Daddy. They're my sons, said Daddy. He brought Andy forward, his hand on Andy's shoulder.

Hey, Sonny, said the man real slow. He looked at Andy for a long time, squinting, going from the bald spot to the ear to his arm. What happened to your hand? he said finally.

Andy looked down at the water. He was in a fire, said Daddy.

Playing with matches? said the man. The sun by then held at the center of the canyon, directly overhead.

No, said Daddy. The color drained down from his temples.

The man looked over at John. It was another boy who had matches, said Daddy quickly, it was an accident, these boys don't play with matches.

Yeah? said the man. He dropped his pole, an expensive bamboo one, and his fancy fish basket into the stream and began to try to get something out of his back pocket. Daddy bent over to get the basket and the pole out of the water, but the man flapped his hand at him to let him know it didn't matter. Finding nothing in his pocket he rubbed himself all over the front of his shirt, but seemed to forget for a while what he was after. I'd have killed my kids if I found them playing with matches, he said, his hands poised over his belly. He began searching again.

He found what he was looking for in the pocket of his

pants: a roll of money. He thumbed through the bills, lots of twenties and tens, deliberating, then tugged at one, releasing it, and leaned over, nearly falling, to stick it in Andy's hand. You better find some other friends, little buddy, he said. He stood up and looked at Daddy out of one eye. What did you do to that kid? he asked. Did you kill him?

Well, said Daddy. He searched along the meadow past the man's head, biting at his upper lip. That boy is our friend, said Daddy quietly. He's one of the boys' good friends. And then a frantic burst of enthusiasm: How long you been up here? Have you caught anything? Where are you from?

Yeah? said the man. He sneezed again, wiping his mouth off with the back of his hand and began to re-consider his money.

Have you caught anything? Daddy said again, a little louder, but the man seemed intent on the roll of bills. Listen, said Daddy, his eye on the money too, these kids don't need money. He took hold of Andy's arm, trying to push him on up out of the stream.

Sure they do, the man went right on counting. Kid can always use a little money. Can't you, buddy? he said looking over at John. Here, he said. He breathed out of his mouth, short and hard. Here's something to buy some candy with. It was a twenty dollar bill. What's the matter, buddy? You can't use a little money? John looked over at Daddy and then at the money Andy had clutched in his hand. He came forward looking down at the stream. The man held the bill out but wouldn't let go of it.

Say, tell me something, pal, said the man, what's this thing you've got covering your face?

These kids don't need money, said Daddy. Come on, John let's go, we have to go on.

Whoa, now, pardner, said the man. Don't get yourself all

worked up. I'm just asking, just curious. Just wanting to know what happened to these poor little fellers. You don't always act like this when people try to do something nice for your kids, do you?

Look, said Daddy, slowly and deliberately, my boy is wearing a mask. He has to wear a mask because he was burned on his face, and burned skin will scar unless you keep pressure on it to keep it flat.

Yeah? said the man. He studied the twenty dollar bill he held in his hand. Well, you know what I always say, said the man, putting the bill back into the roll of money. I always say that nothing is so bad you got to hide it.

Look! exploded Daddy. He's not hiding anything. He has to keep it on. Daddy pushed on John's arm to make him go on, up out of the stream, and looked back at Susie to get her to come follow, but her eye, like John's, was caught by the roll of bills.

What about the girl? said the man, suddenly aware of her. Girl could use a little money, too, couldn't she? Couldn't you, honey? The thumbing through the money began again, that process now at the very center of the canyon, the man studying each shift of his finger, droning on about matches and fires and the way he raised his own kids to be decent, while Daddy, grabbing and pushing, severed Susie and John from the sight and the sound of him, striding out ahead across the high plain toward the car, dragging Andy by the hand.

Daddy had said he would take the kids to Platoro after they fished, to the store in Platoro so they could get some candy, but he turned instead and drove back along the edge of the canyon towards the campsite. He stopped the car finally just short of the pile of firewood, but nobody moved. He stared out over the flat meadow, chewing on his lip, then looked back as if to talk but didn't say anything. Andy still held his treasure tight in his hand where the man had stuck it. Daddy studied it.

How much did he give you? said Daddy. Andy opened his hand but would not look up. Twenty dollars, said Daddy. I want you to share that with your brother and sister, hear? he said and turned back, straight in his seat.

It was hot and no one moved. Finally Daddy said, He was drunk. And said again, after a while, Your mother and I are real proud of you kids. You know that? He turned to look at the three of them. Don't be afraid when people stare, he said, when they ask questions. Just be polite, just do the best you can. He looked down at his hands, empty before him, and then back up at the kids. OK? he said.

We didn't do much the rest of that day, a little fishing, a little gathering of firewood, some half-hearted naps. For supper there were ranchstyle beans and bacon and tortillas. Nobody mentioned the cherry pie that Daddy had planned to buy in Platoro. Daddy and John and Andy stood around the campfire with their hands in their pockets while Susie drew jagged lines in the dirt with a twig.

Whoa, now, pardner, said Daddy suddenly, in a deep slow drawl. The three of them looked over at him. Whoa, now pardner, Daddy drawled again, why ya'll don't always act like this, do you?

Why, no, pardner, said Susie, standing up, brushing herself off. Whenever we see that much money we always act just like this. She froze with her eyes popping out of her head and her mouth wide open. John blinked in amazement. Yeah, he said, just like this, imitating his big sister. Daddy let his jaw drop, too.

Did you see how much money he had, Daddy? shrieked Andy, running over to tug on Daddy and get his attention.

Did I see how much money he had? said Daddy. He flopped down suddenly on the ground and lay like a dead man, with his eyes and mouth gaping open, even the rigors of death unable to erase the astonishment he felt at the drunk man's wealth.

Daddy, Daddy, Daddy, John sputtered, did you see it? Tens and tens and tens and tens and twenties.

I saw a fifty dollar bill, said Susie.

Daddy, said Andy, what if he had given me a fifty dollar bill?

Daddy sat up. He leered at Andy and said, Here you go, little buddy—plunking a rock down in Andy's hand—but you better find yourself a new daddy.

Yeah, said Susie, and while you're at it, pal, get rid of your mother.

And your brother and sister, too, said John.

Move to a new city, pard, said Susie.

Daddy stood up and went outside the circle of the camp-fire where they couldn't see him and came back inside, stumbling along with his eyes down on the ground and aiming straight for Andy. He rammed right into him and fell back, startled, whining, Why . . . Why . . . what happened to your hand, buddy?

His hand! said Susie, and grabbed Andy and turned him around, pointing to his head: This kid is bald.

Yeah, said John, did you notice that this kid is bald?

Why . . . did something happen to your head, little pal? moaned Daddy.

It went on like that for a long time, Daddy playing the drunk man, weaving in and out of the circle, the innocent and guileless cowpoke lurching smack up against that disconcerting vision of Daddy—played by John—in his half-buttoned six-pockets and Susie in her straw hat, of the real John in his mask and Andy without his splint; the wad of money coming in and out of his pocket, dropping from time to time all over the ground, being doled out according to the more or less pitiful merits of the one upon whom he had stumbled, his generosity spun out by Daddy before their eyes so they could squander and spend.

It was nine or past before they could be got into the tent, still talking and laughing and John almost beside himself with the ramifications of the drunk man's eyeful. Susie, Susie, Susie, he kept saying to get her attention, bursting with some new aspect of the case, and it was his voice that we listened to as we sat beside the fire, that stalwart, practical, ancient voice trying to drown out Susie and Andy, suddenly as talkative and confessional as he had been heard but once or twice in his short lifetime.

The moon made its way along the top of the canyon while the three of them talked; we listened, not moving for fear of losing the opportunity. They talked it all through that night, the whole thing, about the party, about Susie's tenth birthday party and how Susie in purple stood at the top of the front steps and waved the boys goodbye as they went to stay at Morgan's house; about how—did Susie remember?—John sat in the back seat with Morgan and had a plate of party cupcakes on his lap. The fort in Morgan's yard had been built the week before of palm branches and an old Christmas tree and John said there were voices in the alley, voices and girls laughing and then the smell of smoke and suddenly the whole thing went up in flames and Morgan ran out and then back and John was stuck on a branch and pulled away and then Andy could not get out, could not get out, and Morgan pulled him out covered with flames.

And threw dirt on him, Susie said. And began to tell it her way. Susie, Susie, Susie, said John, until she shut up.

Listen, he said, it started spreading around. I felt real scared. I felt like I was going to die, except that Morgan found a way for us to get out. So when Andy got out there was fire on his clothes and I felt real scared.

You were stuck inside, said Susie, matter-of-factly.

Listen, Susie, said John, I was already out and I'll tell you what it was like. The easiest part in the whole thing to go through was getting out. And he went on from there, his story: about the plane ride down to Galveston and his eyes and his mouth swollen shut, about Johnson and Jackson in the tub room and how they told jokes and how they always let him watch the TV when they scrubbed him, about the surgeries and the shots and the doctors in their white coats standing in crowds around his bed talking about his face and how they could fix it. And all this time thinking it was the girls laughing in the alley who had thrown a match, just like Morgan told his mother, until Morgan flew down to Galveston and told them how he had seen a book of matches—did they remember?—just before he had come into the fort for the last time and he had struck one and thrown it aside, thinking it was out, and that he hadn't meant to do it and that he was sorry.

Well, Susie wanted to know, what did you tell him, what did you say?

And Johnny said, I said, Sure, OK. But did Susie remember about the time when she had been there when he was finally out of the hospital and they were just waiting for Andy to heal up so they could go home and they all went to the bookstore on the Strand and bought comic books?

Daddy stood up. Um, he sighed and chewed his lip and sat down again for lack of anything else to do while John went on, on and on, remembering only moments of pleasure: the comic books and the Strand and the funny old stores and how Daddy had stood in the middle of the room one night and read *Alice in Wonderland* to him and Andy and Ronnie

Tate and Carnell Hughes. His voice pressed forward steadily, cheerfully from the tent; up above the moon crossed the Pinnacles and then suddenly there was a story we had never heard before, he had never talked about. The first week of school—did Susie remember the first week of school when they finally got back home?—when John had to wear his mask all during school?

Yeah, what about it? Susie wanted to know.

Well, said John, did she know the big boy with the black hair in his class, the one that he had invited to his sixth birthday party whose name he couldn't remember?

Oh yeah, said Susie, that one.

Well, said John, that boy, whatever his name is, made a bunch of the kids who could not speak English take stones and throw them at me.

Oh yeah, Susie said. Did it hurt?

But that was the last Daddy heard, the last thing he listened to. He stood up then and walked away, on up the meadow, as far from the sounds of their voices as he could get.

Daddy brought the Mazda up away from the perfect camping spot exactly one week after he had brought it down and went on a half-day's bumpy ride to descend into the San Luis Valley, there at South Fork where Susie was born, and spent the next hour sightseeing. Here, he said, is the honeymoon cottage and there beside it the road up into the mountains where Mother carried Susie on her back each afternoon, and there the bushes full of rosehips that Mother made into a syrup to feed Susie when she got sick. And there! the bulls that she stood at the window ledge and stared at, the moaning prancing bulls; and o Lord! two buffalo! but of course—every Texas millionaire had a buffalo or two amongst their longhorns. And see! the Rio Grande, crashing around in the back yard, just like I said, Daddy said.

But they hardly listened. Andy fell asleep while Daddy toured the countryside and Johnny read and even Susie after a while was not so interested, ancestral territory or not, and turned down Daddy's offer to drive her by the hospital where she was born. She began to talk about school, about getting ready for school, about notebook paper and pencils and a ring binder and whether or not she would get Mr. Lafarelle for homeroom again. Daddy drove down through Del Norte and on through Monte Vista while she and John made lists of school items and the absolute minimum of clothes that would get them through: 2 pr. jeans, 2 pr. socks, one sneakers, shorts for P.E. The Mazda entered Alamosa and from there passed south, back toward Antonito; the flat plains of Manassa, the quaint stores, even the deep silences of the Sangre de Cristos and the San Juans unnoticed. They were already home. There was school and Sarah and Greg and Jeannie and Junior and John Maxfield and the cat to get back to and it appeared that the trip was over though they still had miles to go.

When He Is Thirty-Seven

W hen he is thirty-seven, it will snow in El Paso. His wife and his children will be in bed. It will be early still, nine or nine-thirty.

At that hour there are clouds lying over the city, pressing down around the mountains at the top of his street. The night is filled with the heavy electric stillness that brings rain. No one expects snow. It is nearly March and the winter has been mild. After supper his kids play outside as if it were summer and in the morning when he goes to work his wife and the woman across the street sit on the front stoop of his house and talk, the way women do at the first sign of spring. In the back yard, the peach tree he planted three years ago, framed in the window of their bedroom, has buds and from the buds faint tokens of the white petals soon to ignite in the brooding air.

He will stay up late, way past midnight. It is a Friday night and from long habit he will drink red wine, sitting down to read at the old dining room table, the newspaper spread out before him, a dim light overhead. He works his tongue in his mouth while he reads just as, were she here to see him, his mother would remember he read as a boy; the same way his son, who is seven, reads now. The paper is full of stories and he leans forward, squinting, letting himself disappear inside them.

But they do not hold him. Then for a long time, he studies the things in this room that is partly a living room and partly a dining room—the couch with the orange and brown stripes in it, the stuffed chair, the unmatched rugs, some pictures drawn by his children and framed carefully by his wife. His son sighs in his sleep. The dog stretches, stands up and shakes, turns around, lies back down on his blanket. The refrigerator clicks on, hums.

He gets up, restless, walking back and forth, goes to the front door and opens it. It is then that he sees the snow. It covers the trees and the bushes, the grass and the side-walks and the houses of all his neighbors—elegant, silent, a special grace.

Are you coming to bed?

His wife calls out sleepily, hearing him as he rummages through the hall closet, looking for the red winter coat and the dark brown wool cap that have been stored there since the days when they lived in colder places, when they were first married. He goes into their bedroom and kneels down beside the bed so he can talk to her.

It's snowing, he says.

It is? Oh no. She smiles, her eyes open for just a minute. For his sake she pretends to raise up on one arm and look out, but she cannot. It's pretty, she murmurs, rolling over onto her stomach.

The red coat buttoned, the collar turned up, the cap cover-ing his ears, he goes outside, standing on the front porch for a long time, looking south toward the lights of Juarez. There are no cars moving on his street. Only an occasional one creeps along the bigger, busier street a block away. Everyone is sleeping, their houses dark and quiet.

Across the street a light comes on. It is Mrs. Miller's house. She is a widow lady. Her nephew, a boy of fifteen or sixteen, has come for a visit from Oklahoma. Now the boy has turned on the light in the glassed-in porch at the side of Mrs. Miller's house, the little crowded corner where she stores newspapers and jars and flowerpots. From where he is standing, the man can see the boy preparing to set out from his aunt's house. The man's wife has told him that Mrs. Miller's nephew is a nice boy, a little too serious perhaps, very shy. Of course, says his wife, that may be because he has no one to hang around with. He is only visiting. Imagine his trying to make friends with the Lopez boys who live two doors away from them. Ha! They are so coarse and rough; they like to drink and swear and sit around talking to girls all night. This boy, Mrs. Miller's nephew, is not like that, his wife has declared.

The boy switches off the porch light so that his aunt won't miss him if she wakes up. He shuts the door carefully behind him. On the top step he buttons his long overcoat. From where the man stands, hidden in the shadows on his front porch, it looks like a good coat, a formal one, the kind that you would bring with you when you visit your aunt because there is no room in your suitcase for two coats and your mother will insist you bring one that will not embarrass your father's older sister, one that will do for church, for shopping, for going out to visit or for play. Although your mother knows that this last is not possible, knows that a boy cannot "play" in a long formal overcoat, knows that a boy cannot consider it when he is visiting his aunt.

It is all right though. For the boy, when he comes to visit his aunt every year, forgoes play of any kind. He stays inside, sleeping late and watching TV. Sometimes he reads and sometimes he helps his aunt cook and sometimes he gives her a hand with the spring cleaning that she likes to save up for when he comes. Though he would never admit it, he likes to be with her, he likes to listen to her talk. Secretly it pleases him to go through his aunt's storage closets in her annual cleanups, to look over the stacks of old magazines she saves and all her old pictures, the funny dated shoes and hats, and to listen to all the old stories that go with them.

There is a great pleasure in hearing his aunt's stories. There is something about people's lives laid out the way his aunt lays them out, like a suit of clothes, that makes him feel as if he is about to understand something very important. The lives she tells about have a beginning and an end, not just an infinite middle, like his own. They can be looked at and studied, conclusions real and fantastic drawn.

But his aunt has her boring moments, too. She is going on sixty-two. She likes to go to bed early. Up alone in her maidenly cottage at night, he feels nervous and restless. He remembers that he is almost sixteen, almost a man. He peers out across the street at the Lopez house where the boys gather in ominous crowds on their front steps. His aunt, he knows, would dislike it intensely if he ever approached the Lopez house where boys of all ages congregate to laugh and curse and make themselves useless. Overcharged with energy, they spill out into the street, playing football or base-ball, depending on the time of year, always screaming and yelling. Every night, late at night, the older boys will sit on the front porch with their girlfriends and tease them. The sound of their excited laughter worries the boy, makes him wish he were older than he is and had more courage than he has.

But tonight the street is silent. The stoop where the Lopez boys crowd by day is covered with snow. Their house is dark.

He is safe then. He walks down the porch steps and out onto the drive, placing his feet down slowly in the clean white snow. At the street he pauses, looking first one way and then another. He sets out toward the main road a block away.

The man watches the boy. Sometimes he is just a dark shadow. Sometimes he is hazy with light and snow, standing beneath the cone of light from the streetlamps. Then for five or ten minutes, Mrs. Miller's nephew is gone.

From out of a side street near his aunt's house, he appears again. He comes to the bottom of her drive. He doesn't want to go in. There is more to do this night. The snow excites him, the silent empty street fills him with power. He starts in the other direction toward the park on the next block but in ten minutes he is back again, his hands jammed into the pockets of his long overcoat, the collar pulled up around his neck.

Now the man, watching the boy, will remember something he had forgotten.

I am sixteen.

I live in Memphis, a river-town.

My father is dead. My mother supports me and my brother and my two sisters by selling real estate.

People want to help us. Is everything all right? they ask. Is there anything we can do? They are always so sad. They fuss over me. How sullen Bobby is, says Uncle John to Mother. Don't you think a boy that age should have a job? Why, when I was his age, I had already been working for five years, helping out my mother and father.

I want to be like my father. Far away from all their voices. Now his life can go on undisturbed. I want to be like him, away from all their voices and all their help. I am sixteen and I don't want any help.

I want to be like my father because he can study life. He is no longer held by it. He can look at it and understand it. A dead man could write a book.

I would like to write a book. I would like to write a book about Memphis and the way it is, about the river, about the black men in the Dew Drop Inn, about Beale Street and the white women in their flowered hats, about the young girls, about my friends, about my friend Walker.

Walker is the only one I can talk to. He walks along down beside the river. He is young and skinny like I am. He stands beside the river and lights a cigarette. He smokes it, the river at his back. When Walker stands beside the river, I can read it, like a book. Where there is an empty space, the river comes to fill it. Where the land will let it, the river moves in. The South is like that, like the river, like a woman. Women are like the river, moving into all the empty spaces that we, through neglect or fear or lack of time, have failed to fill up. The only thing a woman will ignore is a dead man.

My mother is anxious for me to do well in school, to get good grades, to begin to take out the daughters of the best families in Memphis. My mother has the connections through her father that will make a good match possible. But I have already been thrown out of two private high schools and I am not interested in the daughters of good families. I am surly and intractable. In the afternoons Walker and I go down beneath the bridge by the river and drink red wine and smoke Camel cigarettes.

Besides my mother, I have a mammy, Tula. The only ambition that Tula has for me is that I will not worry Mother. A young boy will get hisself into all kinds of trouble, she says to Mother, to soothe her.

Mother and Tula sit up late in the kitchen on Holmes Street that in the afternoon is laced with light and shadow. My mother does not know the kitchen shadows of the afternoon. All day she sells real estate. Her shoulders are stooped. She grinds her teeth in her sleep. She sighs and it rips through us the way a saw might rip through flesh, cutting deep memory in our hearts, tearing at the idea we have sometimes that everything will be all right.

Even after all these years my mother's sighs come to me like blows, heavy and irrevocable. Even after all these years, my mother remarried, a fine house and plenty of money, the sight of her alone, with folded hands, staring straight ahead, makes me afraid.

I am sitting in the kitchen with Tula. I have just turned sixteen. I have my driver's license in the wallet in my back pocket. Outside the clouds lie heavy and pressing over the city, as ominous as women. It will rain.

Do you think Mother will let me have the car? I ask Tula. I watch her hands. She is making biscuits, patting out the dough.

Tula and I sit in the kitchen in the afternoon. She talks to me. She never says anything about my fingers that are yellow from the cigarettes or about my eyes that are sometimes bloodshot or about my friend Walker who Mother says is not a good boy. We do not talk about everyday. She doesn't tell me about her husband she goes to see on Thursdays, her day off, or about her kids. For all we know, we are her kids.

In the kitchen Tula pats the dough and she tells me stories. They are stories that begin when a person is born and end when a person dies. She lays them out like the dough, rolling them flat on the table for me to see and draw my understanding from. She requires nothing from me but that I do not worry Mother.

Where you going? she wants to know.

Caroline Gage is having a party, I tell her, and though she knows I might not go, she is satisfied. She is satisfied because she has no ambition for me other than that I do not worry Mother and Mrs. Gage is Mother's friend. Knowing I was at Caroline Gage's house would bring a certain amount of peace to my mother's heart.

And I haven't lied. Caroline is having a party. Walker and I may even go there. Sometime. Maybe early, maybe late. We cannot tell. It will depend. On how soon we get started, on whether we want to have a beer first, on how much we enjoy driving along in Mother's car, on the black men at the Dew Drop Inn and on the stories they tell. It will depend on whether the night is very fine and if it is, we will go looking for girls. It is spring and the smell of dogwood will drive us nuts and then no stories the black men can tell will hold us at all.

Or, if it rains, maybe we will go to Caroline's.

It is hard to tell.

You be home early, Tula says. Hear? Your mother needs that car.

I watch her hands and do not answer.

Your father wouldn't let you have the car, says Tula. If he was here, he wouldn't let you have the car. She means that if it were up to her, she would not let me have the car, not because she cares one way or the other about it, but because she knows it will worry Mother.

She flours the table and puts the dough down on it, patting it flat. Your mother wanted your daddy to find another job, she begins, as she has begun every time the subject of my father comes up.

She told your daddy she don't like him to fly. And your daddy says he'd quit. He says soon he won't even go up in the air at all, he'd move on to the factory where they make the planes and get him a job as a manager.

She takes a glass and cuts the biscuits out round and separate from the flat sheet of dough.

Said he only have two more times, then he'd quit. That was when Patsy was seven months old. We was in the kitchen, right here, talking about the dinner, waiting for your daddy to come home and the phone ring. They say the plane crashed and your daddy is dead.

She pushes at the last bit of dough.

You crying around the house all day. Daddy. I want my Daddy. Worrying your mother. When you get bigger, when you was five, you never did shut up, you talked all day, you was full of plans. You be in and out of this kitchen all day. Telling me, Tula, I'm going to build a fence. Tula, if we fix the toolhouse this way or that, then we could put more of the rakes in it or more of the hammers. Or how you was going to fix the car. The kind of things a boy tells his daddy, coming in and telling them to me.

She shakes her head back and forth, wiping her hands on her apron.

Can't you walk tonight? she says.

I got my license, I tell her, going to the back door and looking out. I'm a good driver.

I go and sit out on the front porch, waiting for Mother to come home with the car. It is five-thirty and I told Walker that I would be at his house by seven. When Mother gets home, she'll be tired. I'll have to wait awhile before I can ask her to be certain that she'll say yes. I'll have to wait awhile more for her to tell me how important having a car is in the real estate business and how it is real estate that puts food on our table and how she would rather I find another way to go.

I see her drive up the street. My mother is a small woman. I can barely see her head above the steering wheel. She is leaning forward and holding on tightly to it. She pulls into the driveway and her face doesn't relax. It is full of contracts and openings and closings and what will she do to help her children and how will the bills get paid.

It would be so easy to make her laugh. I could say, How

48

are you, Mother? and I could kiss her on her cheek. I could tell her all about myself, about what I want and what I dream of and how well I would like to do in school and the plans I have for my future. But I cannot give her that. Not now, not when I am sixteen and I want the car.

Now all I want is to get away from her, to go out with Walker and get drunk, stay out all night racing up and down the dark wet streets of Memphis in her car.

The car stops by the porch and she sits for a minute, thinking. I don't like to watch her sit and think. I get up and go out.

We carry in the groceries. She is tired and sits down in the living room. Mother, I tell her, Caroline Gage is having a party tonight.

Oh! Oh! she says, as excited as a little girl. I wonder if Ann Gage will want me to send over my punch bowl.

No, I say quickly. She has everything. She said everything is fine.

Well, isn't that wonderful? she says. What will you wear? Your suit?

No, Mother, I tell her. It's not like that. We don't need to dress up.

You need a bath, she says. And a good white shirt.

Yes, Mother, I say. Mother, can I take the car?

Now she is not so excited. I'll drop you over there, she says. And then later, around ten or so, you can walk back.

She gets up and walks out of the room and then comes back. Why, I think that's just marvelous, she goes on. Isn't that nice of Caroline Gage to invite you to her party?

I sit down in the chair in the corner of the room and stare straight ahead of me.

What's wrong with me taking you over, Bobby? she says. That's the only car we've got. That's all we've got.

I only just want to go over there and back, Mother, I say.

Now, all of a sudden, I believe in my story. God, I only just want to get in the car and drive over to Caroline's and come back. You'd think I wanted to go all over Memphis, I yell at her.

No, she says, I can't let you do that.

She sits down in the chair across from me. By now it must be six and Walker will be calling over soon to see what is going on. If Mother knows that Walker is going, I'll never get the car.

I shut my eyes. I know what she is doing, even with my eyes shut. Her hands are clasped and she is rubbing her palms together. She is biting her lip and remembering what Tula remembers and remembering what only she can know. If I look up, if I open my eyes, her eyes will have tears in them. I put my hand over my own eyes to hide from her.

I want you back by eleven, she says finally. At the latest. She sighs. She takes her purse up from beside the chair where it is lying on top of piles of contracts and brochures. She unclasps the handle and searches inside for her keys. I hear them jingle. She turns them over and over in her hands, as if they are beads and she is saying the office of her trials. She holds them out to me. I try not to grab them and run.

You can't go looking like that, she says. You go and clean up. And I'm sure Ann Gage will need the punch bowl. I will get it in its box and get the glasses wiped out and you may carry it over in the car to Caroline's.

I pull out of the driveway at a quarter to seven, the box with the punch bowl and its glasses in the trunk, put there by Mother and Tula. They are standing at the door and watching me. I am wearing a white shirt and have a sport jacket hanging in the back seat and I have promised to be home by eleven and promised to see that Mrs. Gage understands that Mother is in no hurry to have the bowl returned.

*   *   *

Mrs. Miller's nephew shuffles up the sidewalk, his head bent against the snow. He turns back and stares down the street, looking first in one direction and then another. Certain that he is the only one awake at this hour, that the street and the snow are his alone, he begins to run, gathering speed and sliding, making long trails in the untouched snow, falling down and getting up again, dizzy, ecstatic in the sweet dark and empty night.

That night, Walker and I went early to Caroline's, just to get rid of the punch bowl. Mr. Gage was there. He wore a suit and stood at the edge of the living room, checking his watch every few minutes. Mrs. Gage said she was thrilled with the punch bowl. She said that Mother was the most wonderful woman she knew and so brave. Walker and I stuffed ourselves on boiled shrimp and slipped out without saying thank you. It had gotten colder some and the air hung heavy, wrapped around the city like a blanket.

The Dew Drop Inn was packed. After a few beers, me and Walker came out of the back room where you drink if you're white and underage. We sat down in the bar and nobody seemed to care.

An old man sat playing the blues on his guitar. You got to fan it, he sang.

Oh my, yes, said a black woman in a wide-brimmed hat.

You got to fan it to keep it warm, sang the old man, till your baby come home.

The black men were laughing, telling stories, one right after the other, about the women, how they come and go and make them spend, about the work they were doing, working in the white man's yards and houses, about picking up and moving fast, about people living and dying, and Walker and I got drunker and drunker and I forgot all about my promise to Mother to be home by eleven.

The bartender came over after a long while and said, White man coming, boys, to warn us about the cops, and Walker and I got up and went out the back door, but it was a whole different night outside than the one it had been when we'd first come in.

It had snowed. Goddamn! yelled Walker and we stood, leaning against the back of the Dew Drop Inn, and stared at it for a long time. Then we peed and got into Mother's car and drove ever so slowly out of the alley behind the Dew Drop Inn where we always parked and set out through town, slowing down even more to stare into the empty stores, leaning out of the windows of Mother's car to look with astonishment at the long empty lunch counters where there were no people. The streets were empty, the sidewalks were empty, everything was covered with snow and Walker and I were so drunk, we were astounded.

The clock over a pawnshop said it was twenty to two.

My God, Walker, I said to him. Mother will kill me. I've got to hurry home.

Yeah, he said, hurry.

We got onto Central, heading east, away from the river. It had two or three inches of snow on it and, for as far as we could see, it was wide and straight and empty.

Hurry, hurry, Walker said. I pressed down a little on the gas to get up some speed. Not too much in case someone should see us and think we were drunk. But I was so anxious suddenly about Mother's car that I slammed down on the brakes. The car began to spin. I heard Walker moan. The back end came around to where the side was and Walker and I turned in surprise to watch it. It spun slowly, as if it were in a dream, and when it came to rest, we were heading west again toward the river.

I thought we were going to die, Walker said.

So did I, I told him.

See if you can do that again, he said. Spin around the other way.

I got the car going fast, maybe a little too fast, because when we spun the next time, it turned full circle and we were right back where we started.

Here, said Walker, let me try it. He got out of his side and I got out of mine. We stopped for a minute to pee again in the fresh snow. He lit a cigarette and got behind the wheel.

Okay, he said.

That night Walker and I spun all the way down Central, taking turns, going first in one direction and then in the other, getting up some speed and slamming on the brakes. We must have spun thirty or forty times that night in Mother's car, going all the way down Central to home.

The boy is beginning to get cold. The spell of the snow and the quiet night is over for him. He trudges up the street, toward home. The bed in his aunt's house will be warm and he is ready to go back to sleep.

The light at the side of Mrs. Miller's house comes on. It is Mrs. Miller, holding the neck of her bathrobe closed, peering out. She sees her nephew coming up the drive and opens the side door for him. The man can almost hear what she is saying. Can imagine it, anyway.

The boy and his aunt stand face to face on the glassed-in side porch while Mrs. Miller finds out where he has been and what he has been doing. The man can see the two of them talking, the boy sleepy, his aunt wondering if it is all right to believe what he has told her. She turns to look out across the street, toward the Lopez house, anxious to see if they are up. Satisfied that they are not, she turns back.

The light on her porch goes off. Lights appear throughout the house while Mrs. Miller adjusts herself to this strange whim of the nephew she thought she knew so well and while the boy, not caring if she believes him or not, falls asleep.

The last light goes out in Mrs. Miller's house. The street lies silent and dark, no cars to wake it, no commerce to engage it. The man stands quietly on his porch, watching, thinking about his mother, and then now his own children, letting his memories and his dreams, like the snow, drift down slowly and surround him.

Hotter Here Than It Ever Was
in New Jersey

The lady who said she was from Tupelo wore pink bedroom slippers and a too-short dress stretched taut and ragged across her swollen knees. She was rehearsing the recent agonies of her granddaughter for a woman who sat across from her in a close and narrow waiting corridor, a woman with brown hair who said she lived in El Paso but took pains to note that she had not been born there but was born instead in New Jersey. NEW JERSEY, she said twice.

Not interested in where the brown-haired woman came from or why it was important for her to mention it more than once, the lady from Tupelo labored through the details of her granddaughter's ordeal in a drawl as flat and indifferent as if she were talking about the offspring of some Chinaman who lived in the furthest reaches of Siberia and not her very own flesh and blood. She punctuated the more gruesome items with a tap-tap-tapping from an umbrella she held in her left hand, a ruffled black taffeta affair that had long ago lost its shine and many of its spokes.

Beside her in a chair at either bulging arm sat a vacant, rawboned couple, a man and woman whose complexions were as pale and ashen as cooked pork. Both of them were preoccupied with smoking.

The sun outside the thin hospital window was set for noon in May, pitched directly overhead, hard and yellow. The narrow waiting corridor baked in its glare and reeked of the dark secret odors of hidden unwashed flesh and greasy food which for the woman from New Jersey most assuredly constituted the very essence of Tupelo.

I went to town, was how the fat grandmother from that city had opened suddenly, immediately after she and the New Jersey woman had established their respective places of residence and birth. It being the first of the month and her daughter eligible for welfare and food stamps.

Had to go. Couldn't trust them to go alone, she said, squinting narrowly at the woman with the brown hair so as to shut the rawboned couple out of her vision. The boy-friend was no good. Had been in jail twict and couldn't be trusted with money. Her own daughter didn't have no sense. The things she could tell. Tap. Tap. Tap.

She sighed. They left the granddaughter at home alone. She was seven. Plenty big enough to be left alone. Plenty big enough to know how to cook. Big enough to know how to turn on the oven by herself.

Anyways she was sick with a fever and the chills. She stayed in bed. She had on her pink nightgown, the one they give her for her birthday, from the K-Mart.

They had them this lady next door. A nigra woman with a big mouth. This nigra woman had a big black buck who come and beat her up a few nights a week. Tap. Tap. Tap.

They both was in the house next door at the same time that the granddaughter stood up to try to warm herself from the chills in front of the oven in her pink nightgown.

The woman with the brown hair who was born in New Jersey did not quite see the relationship between these two events. She scowled.

The Tupelo lady said that it would be a matter for the police to be investigating. As soon as them doctors found out for sure whether the girl would live or die they were going to look her over to see if that black buck had touched her. Tap. Tap. Tap. Because from what the nigra lady said, it had been the black buck who first seen her come out on the front porch of their house, spinning and screaming and all on fire. That's what the nigra with the big mouth told the police. But there weren't no black buck around anywhere by the time the Tupelo lady got home with her daughter and daughter's worthless boyfriend and the four sacks full of groceries. And the granddaughter couldn't tell them nothing. She was half burnt to death.

The lady from Tupelo wiped her face off with a dirty piece of Kleenex she held tight in her hand.

The nigra next door was the stupidest nigra the Tupelo lady had ever met. When her and her daughter and the daughter's worthless boyfriend had come back from town, the nigra could hardly tell them what had happened or where the granddaughter had gone or why the house smelled like smoke.

She's gone, the Tupelo lady whined, imitating her stupid neighbor. Your girl is gone.

Where's she gone? they demanded of her.

Don't know, the nigra had wailed. Didn't tell me, but she gone. Gone in the am-bu-lance.

They called the police and the police finally come and took them to the hospital. They had the si-reen on. The umbrella struck the floor while the fat lady from Tupelo raised her neck and howled to demonstrate the truth of that very fact.

There was a bunch of doctors. One after another. There

was a little-bitty doctor who had no hair on his head and he said the granddaughter was burnt inside and out.

There was one who was a Jap and he said she was going to die that day. Said she was burnt thirty-six.

There was one even who was a nigra. A fe-male! And she said they were going to have to fly the girl to the charitable hospital for burns in Galveston, Texas, in whose sweltering third-floor waiting room they now all sat. The lady from Tupelo and her daughter and the daughter's worthless boyfriend. And the woman with the brown hair from New Jersey.

But they didn't fly the girl that same day. Mostly what they did was to keep them all sitting there in that hospital in Tupelo way past suppertime. And they were getting tired, too. The grandmother got aholt of the Jap and told him about being so hungry and so tired and having nothing but food stamps for money and he took them down to the cafeteria and bought them some supper.

She didn't care what they said about Japs.

Fried chicken and ladypeas and mashed potatoes and black bottom pie for dessert. And then he called the police and they come and drove them home. And hardly before they even got to sleep, the police car come back to get them and take them to the airport. Dark it was and still nighttime and them with just the clothes they had on and a change of underwear and a couple of sandwiches in a paper sack. And the frigerator back in Tupelo full of food from the food stamps and them not having any idea how long all this would take.

One of them private jets flew them all down to Galveston. The granddaughter had a nurse. The girl was wrapped in white bandages all over. All over her hands and her legs and her head and her face. And she smelled. Lord. Gawd. The whole airplane was filled with her smell.

The umbrella clattered to the floor. The lady from Tupelo shut her eyes and stopped talking as abruptly as she had started.

The woman with the brown hair who was born in New Jersey tapped her faded red sandals impatiently on the floor. She fished around in the bottom of her purse for an old wristwatch she always carried that had no buckle on the strap. A quarter to one. In ten minutes she could go to her son's room and take him out on his first pass, but for now she would have to sit here. There was no point in going somewhere else. Though she might have chosen different circumstances for herself than the ones that presently surrounded her.

The hospital cafeteria was on the next floor down. She could probably go there if she really wanted to get away. But it was closed already. She wasn't hungry anyway. And she'd already drunk enough coffee to sink a ship.

She could go down and talk to the psychologist.

But there was nothing really to talk about.

Now there definitely had been a time when there was PLENTY to talk about. She would be the first to admit that. PLENTY. And she had talked and talked and talked and talked. But that time was past. She had accepted the fire completely. She knew that the next step was to stand beside her boy while he faced the world. And since she was right now on the very brink of that next step, there was really no place else to go but right here, exactly where she was, whether she happened to care for the circumstances or not.

She eyed the strange trio sitting across from her. The grandmother looked like she had fallen asleep. That was fine with the woman from New Jersey. She had no desire to hear any more about the Tupelo granddaughter. And the vacant couple was so intent on smoking they didn't even notice her staring at them.

Trash, she thought, pursing her mouth up. This hospital was full of them. Poor. Slovenly. Stupid. Wondering whether a black man had touched their child when the girl was half burned to death. Worried about the food in their refrigerator and how long all this would take.

Soon these people would be just like the rest of the trash here. Fascinated by the details of each case on the Acute Ward. Sitting around all day and talking. Talking in the halls. Talking outside the rooms. Talking in the elevator. They always took the elevator.

That kid there been burned all over his body. Ninety-two. Should of died. Nurse said so.

You seen that little niggah boy? Don't have no mama. Mama done left. The daddy's girlfriend stuck that kid in a tub full of boiling water. She in jail for the reeeest of her life.

See that little-bitty baby. You seen that poor little baby by itself in the big room? Bless its heart. Its mama and daddy take drugs. Nurse said so.

The woman from New Jersey glared at the Tupelo contingent, tugging at the strands of washed-out red glass beads around her neck. That was exactly the sort of thing they'd say, exactly the sort of thing that would occupy them for the next however-many months, while the food rotted in their refrigerator in Tupelo. Where do these sort of people come from? she thought to herself. They are so stupid. They don't understand anything.

Suddenly the grandmother's eyes popped open and she began again. She smelt like burnt meat, she said. That whole airplane smelt like burnt meat. I got sick, couldn't hardly stand it. Later I seen her chest, looks like a slab of raw beef. She got fire on her face, too. Doctor says she going to have scars all over her. Ain't no man ever want to touch her, that's one thing.

The woman from New Jersey looked away, out the window. The lady from Tupelo made her sick. She was fat and she smelled. The daughter and her worthless boyfriend made her sick, too. The hospital made her sick. The blue and yellow rooms. The close waiting corridors. The smells of dressings and diapers and flesh. The halls always full of burned children, racing up and down, dirty and unruly. As if they'd given up caring what people thought about them. As if their lives were over. As if now that their lives were over they could do whatever they damn pleased. Spoiled! Rotten! Just like that food in the refrigerator in Tupelo would be by the time these people got back. Just thinking about it made the woman from New Jersey sick.

Her boy was not spoiled. Not her boy. Not her Carl. Burned or not, he was different. Had been different before. Was going to be different. Not like the rest of them.

Carl was well-mannered and polite. He was always clean. The woman from New Jersey saw to that. His clothes were going to be brand-new. Though they might have to go in debt to get them. She touched the shopping bag beside her chair. It was full of boxes. New slacks. A new shirt. A new pair of socks. And new brown shoes. It would be obvious to people what kind of boy he was. Anyone that tidy was a good boy and a nice boy and people would like him for that. He would not get treated like the rest of these children were bound to get treated. Oh, she knew. The psychologist had spoken to her many times about how burned children were received out in the world. Yes, she understood that. She had come to terms with that. She knew there might be some difficulty. But she was also confident that, with her help, Carl would fit right back into things nicely.

Now the rest of these children. She couldn't answer for any of them. They may have been bad children to start. Bad children from bad and broken homes, where their parents, if they had any, didn't give a fig what they did or who they played with. If they had cared, their children never would have gotten burned.

Carl never would have gotten burned if their garage hadn't caught on fire. And he wasn't the one who set it on fire, she said to herself slowly and mechanically, as she had said before a million times to what seemed to be a million inquiries. It was nobody's fault. It was an accident. He doesn't play with matches.

She was not like these other parents. These other parents obviously didn't love their children. They just left them to raise themselves. Now all of a sudden all they could think about was how their kids looked. Why, just this morning in the parents' weekly conference with the doctors she had heard a mother—a scrawny unkempt girl whose sweat smelled as if she'd been taking drugs—ask in a thin and whining voice where her boy could go to school now that no one would look at him anymore.

God! She tugged at the end of her fingernail with her teeth. This is 1981, she said, lecturing to the whole lot of these foolish parents in her imagination. This is 1981, not the Dark Ages. You don't need to hide your children. Times have changed. If you will just change your own attitude. If you will just look and see that you have not raised your children properly. If you will just tidy them up, keep them presentable, teach them to be well-mannered, and change your own attitude . . .

She considered again the roster of things that she had planned for that afternoon. It would make a good example—if anyone cared to listen—of the sort of thing these people could do to help their children toward recovery. It was a good idea, this pass, and was highly recommended by the doctors and psychologists as very very therapeutic. An opportunity to get out and test your wings before you were actually released from the hospital for good.

First she and Carl would walk down the three flights of stairs. That would be good exercise for him, as it was for every person here, a healthy alternative to the elevator. They would stop at the front desk, to show the receptionist how nice he looked in his new clothes. The receptionist was a lively young college girl who was always asking how Carl was doing.

From there they would walk to Baskin-Robbins for an ice cream cone, then on to the beach and a possible stroll down beside the water. Then home to the apartment she had rented so that Carl could see where she had lived these last three months.

Now these were the kind of wholesome activities that a child who had undergone so much . . .

What's the number of your kid? asked the lady from Tupelo, leaning forward.

The woman from New Jersey frowned. She had almost completely forgotten the flesh-and-blood fat lady across from her while she'd been delivering her little talk to her and others like her in her imagination.

You got a kid here, said the lady from Tupelo. I seen you here this morning.

Yes, said the brown-haired woman. She folded her hands together on her lap and tapped her red sandal on the floor.

Do you mean what room is he in or what percent of his body was burned? That's what you mean, don't you? It's called the percentage. What percentage of his body was burned? she said, talking very quietly and carefully.

The lady from Tupelo blinked.

My son, continued the woman from New Jersey, was burned over 62 percent of his body.

Yeah? said the lady from Tupelo. My granddaughter got 70.

The woman from New Jersey crossed her arms over her chest. I thought you said it was 36 percent, she said.

Yeah, said the Tupelo lady.

Well, what is it? Is it 36 percent or 70 percent? Because there's a big difference. The brown-haired woman sat up very straight in her chair. Is it all third degree?

It's bad, said the Tupelo lady.

The woman from New Jersey fussed with the creases in her seersucker skirt, pushing at them nervously with her hand. Her ankle wiggled of its own accord. A single thread of sweat unexpectedly made its way down along the underside of her arm.

My son is burned almost entirely third degree, she said suddenly, the words exploding from her. She glowered at the lady from Tupelo, trying to hold that person's watery eyes with her own, but the lady from Tupelo looked right past her. That's the maximum amount of burn there can be, she pushed on, but deliberately now, precisely. That's all three layers of skin. Sixty-two percent. Now that's bad.

Yeah? said the lady from Tupelo. She shut her eyes.

He is burned on the top of his head, continued the woman from New Jersey, on the left side of his face, on his left arm, on his back and on his chest. He lost his ear and three fingers.

The Tupelo lady's head slipped forward a little, as if she were just catching herself from falling asleep.

He's bad, said the brown-haired woman, just a little louder than she had intended to before. She tried to get the attention of the daughter and the daughter's boyfriend, but their eyes wouldn't connect with hers.

Sixty-two percent, all third degree, is bad, she said again. He's been in the hospital for three months. For over three months. And I've been here with him the whole time. I had to leave my whole world behind me.

No one seemed interested. The daughter's worthless boy-friend put his hand in his breast pocket and took out another cigarette in a motion so slow that the brown-haired woman was arrested by it. When he finally lit the match, she felt as if he'd struck it on her insides, it surprised her so, and she jumped and pushed ahead, now fully irritated.

I went in to see him right away, right after the fire, long before they flew him here in the private plane, she said. My husband—she said it emphatically as if the word might have no meaning to her audience—was with me that whole first month. Then he had to go back to work. We just could not afford to have him out of work for more than a month. He works, she said pointedly. In El Paso.

When I first saw my son, his skin was falling off in strips and it was yellow. And when they took him into the tubs to take the skin off, I could hear him screaming. Now he was one they thought would die. He was bad.

The woman from New Jersey took a long, deep breath. She rubbed her face with both her hands.

But your granddaughter, she said finally, if she is indeed burned over 36 percent of her body, is going to be fine. Thirty-six percent is nothing.

But they didn't seem to care. The vacant couple kept on smoking. The fat lady was preoccupied with the Kleenex she held clutched in her hand.

The brown-haired woman laid her head back against the wall. She shut her eyes, exhausted. And dozed off, or must have. Carl's face flew before her sleeping mind, the left eye drawn down to his chin, the mouth twisted up by his fore-head. No! She woke up suddenly, sweating. That's not what he looks like!

Which one is he? The lady from Tupelo was asking her a question. She was leaning forward and squinting at her out of one eye.

The brown-haired woman looked out the window, across the street, trying to get her mind settled, trying to figure out where she was and what this lady across from her wanted. Finally it all came into focus. He's in the first room, she said slowly.

Yeah? said the lady from Tupelo.

His name is Carl, said the brown-haired woman after a while.

Yeah? said the lady from Tupelo again. She dabbed at her lip with the rumpled Kleenex. He the one that wears that thing over his face? Just sits there on the end of his bed? First room?

Yes, said the brown-haired woman. She sat up straight. Only he is not just sitting there. Sometimes he watches TV. He watches many educational programs. You can't see the type of show he is watching from the hallway.

Why's he wear that thing? asked the Tupelo lady.

That's a mask. All the children wear masks if they are burned on their faces. Haven't you seen any of the other children wearing masks?

The lady from Tupelo sniffled.

Well, said the brown-haired woman, the masks are a major breakthrough in burn care. A very major breakthrough.

The Tupelo lady looked at her sullenly.

Your granddaughter will have to wear a mask, said the woman with the brown hair. She tried hard to look very serious. Just like my son. Just like everyone else.

That so? said the lady from Tupelo. She crossed her arms up over her chest. She didn't say anything at all. And then, suddenly, How'd he get burned?

The brown-haired woman sat back in her chair. He was in a garage fire, she said. It was nobody's fault, it was an accident.

My girl wasn't playing with no matches, said the Tupelo lady. She knows how to light the stove.

Well, said the woman with the brown hair. My boy doesn't play with matches either.

The two women stared at each other.

The lady from Tupelo spoke first. Nurse said this morning that a little boy died here awhile back. She sat up particularly straight. Didn't die from no fire, just died from being here. Nurse said onct an infection starts can't nothing stop it. Kills people. Everybody dies, even the doctors.

The woman with the brown hair scowled at the Tupelo lady's pink bedroom slippers. Her toenails were yellow and dirty and long.

The Tupelo lady sighed, an enormous sawing noise. I got a bad heart, she said. Had a heart attack last year.

The brown-haired woman's red sandal slapped against her foot.

My girl here can't work. She's got to take care of her kid. They're giving us a room in the Holiday Inn and giving me and the girl seven dollars a day for food. They got king-size beds over there and a twenty-four-inch color TV. Don't know what they're going to do about him. Said they couldn't pay for more than me and the girl because we're kinfolks.

Well, said the brown-haired woman.

A door across from the narrow waiting corridor opened up. A nurse dressed in a pink uniform looked at the woman from New Jersey and said, Your son is ready for you now.

Well, said the brown-haired woman, standing up. I have to go. My son is ready for me. They're giving him a pass today so he can go outside for a while and see what things are like. He hasn't been outside for three months.

She picked up the shopping bag full of new clothes. I guess I'll be on my way, she said. We're really going to go out on the town, she said a little too gleefully for her own comfort. The ice cream parlor. The beach. Walking down the seawall. My apartment. I better get going because we've really got some things to do, she said.

But instead she stood in the corridor for a minute longer, biting on her lip.

The Tupelo lady dabbed at her face with the last worn bit of Kleenex and stared at the floor.

I think your daughter, your granddaughter, will be fine, said the woman from New Jersey, feeling for a minute as if she had been unkind to these people. I think that the first couple of weeks is the worst, she went on. I remember that my first couple of weeks here were the worst I'd ever spent. I didn't know if Carl would live or die. But it gets better.

They could hear a door down the hall opening and shutting impatiently.

Well, let me qualify that, said the brown-haired woman quickly, her eye on the hallway. It gets better until you realize that your child will have scars. Her voice got lower. Now that is really the worst part. But even that gets better. You come to terms with it. You accept it. You get a handle on it and after a while it hardly bothers you anymore.

The trio from Tupelo listened to this extraordinary capsulization of the New Jersey woman's experience without showing any sign whatsoever of having heard or understood it. She waited for them to comment, but they didn't say a word.

Well, okay, she said finally. She stood staring down at them for a minute and then turned and made her way along the hall toward Carl's room very slowly, feeling dizzy and not even half as eager to take him out on a pass as she had felt before she had met the people from Tupelo.

Suddenly the trip seemed absurd. Two hours out in the hot sun with a boy who was wearing a mask? Who had been lying in a hospital bed for three months? Just so people could see him? It didn't make a single shred of sense.

She leaned against the wall just outside of Carl's room. The blinds were drawn on his door, but she saw him peering through them looking for her.

Mom? she heard him say. And there he was, standing at the door. He was wearing only underpants, his legs and arms wrapped with Ace bandages, his hands swaddled in splints and more bandages, his head covered with a tight brown hood, like a stocking, that held a white life mask in place. With the mask on, she could only see his eyes and his mouth. His lips were swollen out from the pressure of the mask on his face. The sight of his frail, broken body, now just barely seven years old, struck her with such an overpowering measure of pain that her eyes filled full of tears and her heart felt as if it would burst loose from her. But he did not notice.

Did you bring my clothes? was his first question. And his second, right behind the first, Did you buy the shoes I wanted?

The questions brought her back to the trip at hand. She walked swiftly across the room, putting her shopping bag down on his bed. The room was empty, except for the two of them, the other children—older than Carl—having been allowed to forgo their afternoon naps in favor of a game of pool in the playroom down the hall. From Carl's room, she could see past the nurse's station to the rooms opposite his. Younger children lay sleeping in their beds and in their cribs, shrouded in white sheets. In one room, white curtains surrounded a single bed. The lights were dimmed and nurses and doctors were going in and coming out. A new case. An acute burn. Probably the Tupelo lady's granddaughter, the New Jersey woman concluded.

She and her son spoke in whispers, even though they were alone. Here is a new shirt, she said quickly. I just went to the department store in the Holiday Mall and bought it this morning. Green and blue check. You always like green and blue.

A new shirt! He sank down on the bed. What about the one I asked you to bring? What about the one Dad was going to mail over here?

Look, she said. Don't start that. Your father didn't have time to mail it or any of your other clothes. He has to work. And even if he had mailed it over here, it wouldn't be right. This is an occasion for a new shirt, no matter how much it costs. Although I did get this one on sale.

He stood stiffly while she pushed his arms into the sleeves. Your first day out of the hospital, she cooed. Don't you want to look nice?

It's too small, he said.

No, she said. It's just right. And here are the pants. They were dress pants, made of polyester, in a gray blue to pick up the blue in his checkered shirt.

He groaned. Couldn't you have asked Dad just to mail my old jeans?

You have gotten fatter, she said firmly. You wouldn't be able to wear your old jeans even if your father had sent them. Now stand up.

Why didn't you buy me some new jeans then?

These are just like new jeans, she said, touching his leg so he would raise it.

New jeans! he sputtered. These are like something you go to church in.

Well, she said, pursing her mouth together. This is a special occasion. Like going to church, she added, grimly. I want you to look nice. Don't you want to look nice?

I don't look nice, he cried. I'm not going to wear this stuff.

Yes you are.

I'm not going.

Listen, she said, grabbing onto his shoulders. When you leave this hospital, you are going to go out looking decent. Do you hear me? She shook him. You will not look sloppy. You will not look poor. You are not poor, do you understand? Your father is working hard to make a good living, she said, forcing the shirt into his pants. She snapped them shut and zipped the zipper. There. We may not have a whole lot of money but we are not poor people, she said. Now sit down while I put your socks and shoes on.

The socks were dress socks, and the shoes were brown. He had wanted sneakers and gray athletic socks, and they argued again. He cried until the eyes of his mask were wet.

The woman from New Jersey sat down on the edge of her son's bed. She felt so tired. This trip made no sense at all. The boy cried on and on. Her nerves were sore and aching. She wanted to scream. She couldn't go anywhere like this. Maybe she could just lie back and shut her eyes for a minute, just to collect her thoughts. He might not even notice.

Her head hit his pillow and she was asleep, resting there in the dark cool room until the noise of his crying stopped and was replaced by his voice talking. He was telling himself things—this and that—walking around the room, suddenly entranced by the fact that he was alone there in that place that was usually occupied by four other boys vying for the TV and the nurses' attention. But not entirely alone. His mother lay asleep on his bed.

Here is Ronnie Tate's bed, she heard him say and she could see him even as she slept, as she knew he would be, standing reverently at the end of the bed of this young black boy who had not ceased to receive the weekend adorations of his many aunts and uncles since the day he arrived. They had come bearing silver dollars and baseball cards and bags of candy and movie magazines and pinup posters and comic books. And now the time was ripe for a close look, the room empty and Ronnie Tate safely down the hall, playing pool. Carl must have moved up by Ronnie Tate's nightstand for here the catalog began and she could hear it, just faintly, like soft music, like a list of things she had always wanted.

Here is the jar of money. Silver dollars. Dimes. Quarters. Nickels. Pennies. Almost full. Hmmm. Here are the baseball cards he got last week. A baseball. Signed by the Dodgers. Wonder Woman. Batman. Michael Jackson.

The woman from New Jersey was rocked into a deep sleep by the sound of her son's voice as it moved all along the edges of that room. Here is Carnell Hughes's bed. He has surgery on Tuesday. He says he doesn't need it. Hmmm. Trays from lunch. Ronnie didn't eat his apple.

She had a dream. Her husband was secretly building her a new house even while they were still living in their old house. She said she didn't need a new house, but he said that the old house was ruined. It was no longer useful, he told her. He took her to see the new house and it was almost finished, down to the curtains and the furniture. But it was odd. She didn't quite like the fact that it was way way out in the middle of the desert, a place that was all flat empty desert and dark gray mountains. But even there, even way out there, there were many strange houses crowded up against it. And no wonder! The house was purple and orange. She wanted to look inside, just like everyone else was doing.

As she pressed up against the front windows, she saw that there at her dining table—which was just like the tables in the cafeteria across the street from the hospital—were three men in pinstripe suits and white shirts and shiny dark silk ties. They were the same men who sat in the cafeteria every morning when she ate her breakfast. They were staring at their shoes and they were all three of them dead. You could tell. You could just tell. The black waitress who worked in that same cafeteria was waiting on these dead men. She came over to the table with plates of biscuits. One of the dead men grinned and said, Ain't no man ever going to want to touch her.

And then one of the other ones said, We can't hire him. I don't care how smart he is, or how much better he is than us. We can't hire anyone with a face like that. The third dead man stared down at his polished shoes and said, Not with a face like that. He might as well be dead.

The woman from New Jersey groaned in her sleep, sweating, trying to get inside that new house that her husband had built her and tell those dead men that they were dead, tell them a thing or two about her son's face, but she could not get in at all and they just kept right on talking as if they were absolutely and positively the only ones who had the answer. And then she heard her son's voice again, was aware of it, going over and around the dream and he was still cataloging things but they were different now, not other people's, but his own.

This is a mask, he was saying. Here is my ear. She opened her eyes. He was standing by Ronnie Tate's nightstand again and he had found a mirror.

Yes, he was saying, I have lost some hair. Third degree. Yes, second degree. It was swollen shut and I couldn't eat. My ear is gone too. And some fingers.

Carl? she said. He turned to look at her.

Are you ready? she said. The short nap had given her new energy. It would be all right to go ahead with this excursion, to go on out and see what it would be like. After all, it was just a mask.

Why, we all of us walk around wearing masks, hiding from each other!

And he had just been in an accident and he just needed to wear the mask so that his skin would stay smooth. That was so easy to understand. Everyone would. And he was going to get better, much better, and his face would be normal and people would accept him and he would grow up and go to college and get a job and get married, just like everyone else, and no one would ever know that anything at all had happened to him.

And really, his face hadn't been burned half so bad as some of the kids she had seen. He looked pretty good in comparison to them. She sat up.

And really, it wasn't all that hot outside.

Ready to go? she said cheerfully. Don't you think we ought to go? Have I been asleep a long time? She got down off the bed. We're going to have fun. Ice cream and a walk along the beach. And you get to see my apartment. And you get to go outside and feel the sun and the air and see the ocean.

Do we have to walk?

Of course we have to walk. What do you think we are? she teased him. Rich? Do you think we have our own chauffeur-driven Rolls-Royce? Huh? And look! You have new shoes.

They hurt.

Of course they don't hurt. I matched them up exactly against the picture I drew of your foot, she said, although that wasn't exactly true. She had matched them up exactly against the picture but she hadn't even considered the Ace bandages that were secured under his feet.

The socks are too thick.

She hadn't thought about the socks either.

It's too hot, he said.

She was quickly losing her resolve again and it irritated her. It is not too hot, she said in a much too patient voice. Your shoes fit and so do your socks. And you stop this right now! You're acting like a spoiled brat. She walked around the room gathering up her purse, putting away the boxes and paper sacks. She went into the bathroom to fix a cold rag to wipe his face after he took his mask off at the ice cream parlor. She wrung it dry and put it in a plastic sack and tried to imagine that things would be okay. If she just kept on getting ready. *Despite* the fact that his shoes were too small and his socks were too thick and the sun was too hot. Despite the fact that the clothes and the bandages would suffocate him. Despite the fact that the trip, the trip itself, would take them—in those too tight shoes and too thick socks—forever.

He was sitting on the bed with his shoulders slumped when she came out of the bathroom. She could feel sorry for him but if there was one thing she would not stand for, it was for him to feel sorry for himself.

Come on, she said, jerking him up by the elbow. We're going, heat or no heat, shoes or no shoes. We're going if you have to go barefoot.

His slender body stiffened under her tight hand.

Get going! she said, pushing him. I haven't got the time to fool with you. He began to cry again and it made her even more angry. She shoved him across the room and out into the bright, sunlit hallway and it was there that she heard the flat lifeless drawl of the lady from Tupelo once more. She remembered her and the vacant cancerous pair as if she had met them many years ago in a dream.

She pressed her nails into Carl's bony arm so hard that he winced. You straighten up, she whispered loudly. Do you hear me? Now there are people down the hall, and their granddaughter was just in a fire. They don't understand what's happened to them. She put her hand in the middle of his back to keep him going in the right direction.

You be nice to this lady. She's big and fat. And the people she's with are very strange. And don't you dare stare at them or say anything at all about them. Do you hear me?

He nodded solemnly, unable to say a word. The eyes of his brown hood were rimmed with tears.

Take a deep breath, she said.

The woman from New Jersey gave her son Carl a final push down the hallway toward the narrow waiting corridor, gritting her teeth tighter and tighter as they drew nearer to the monotonous voice of the lady from Tupelo. Then they were there, standing right in front of them.

Hello, said the woman from New Jersey. She smiled carefully. Here I am again. And here's my son, Carl. She put her arm around him.

The people from Tupelo leaned back, leaning away from them. Not all at once. Not quickly. But ever so slowly. And their eyes grew bigger the further away they got. The woman from New Jersey couldn't believe how frankly they stared. Here he is, she said again. This is Carl.

They did not say a word but only sat there, gawking. It confused the woman from New Jersey so that she suddenly felt like she did when she drank more than three cups of coffee before breakfast, like she couldn't figure out what she was thinking, like she couldn't make any sort of decision of any kind. She gave her head a little quick hard shake and pressed ahead, hoping for some response other than the one she was getting.

Carl, she said, very politely, this lady is from Tupelo. That's in the state of Mississippi. Her granddaughter was in a fire. Yesterday. Yesterday? Is that correct?

The fat lady didn't answer. She kept squeezing and turning the dirty Kleenex in her hand.

You going to let him go out with that thing on? she said suddenly.

The woman from New Jersey winced. This is his mask. She tried to whisper, thinking that this was really something she didn't want discussed in front of Carl, but he was peering up at her and not missing a word.

Don't you remember that I was telling you about it? she

asked them. Your granddaughter will wear one of these too.

Their eyes roamed over every inch of Carl's body, from the top of the brown hood to the flat red emptiness of his missing ear to the piece of matted hair that stuck out from behind the mask to the splints that covered his hands, down over all his new clothes.

The woman from New Jersey watched them stare at Carl with a sort of fascination, looking therein for some understanding. And then she had it. She was suddenly absolutely certain that they did not understand about the mask. That was it. It was just the mask that frightened them. It was the mask that horrified them. Not Carl. Her stomach was filled with excitement. Though perhaps it wasn't the right time to do it, nor really the right place, neither was it anyone's business—especially the business of the people from Tupelo— she felt uncannily certain that they ought to see the face beneath the mask. Then they would see how good he looked. And they wouldn't be frightened anymore. They would stop staring and she and Carl could go on.

Her fingers reached up toward the back of Carl's head, shaking, to the velcro closing at the back of the hood, and pulled it open hard. It startled the boy and he cried out. She turned him around toward her and said, Ssshhh, ssshhhh, and whispered, I just want to show them your face, how good it looks. And pulled up on the hood and then it was off. She leaned in and looked at him hard.

The boy rubbed his eyes, as if he'd been asleep beneath the mask all that time. The woman from New Jersey brushed his face free of little bits of hair that clung to it and took the edge of her sleeve and tried to dry the sweet sickly-smelling sweat off of it. And then turned him around so the people from Tupelo could be reassured, turned him around so they could see him in the full light of the corridor's window.

Now, she said. See how wonderful he looks. Can't you see how wonderful he looks? she said, addressing the wall above their heads, not quite looking into their eyes.

The fat lady sucked in hard.

Gawd, she said.

Why, you can't even imagine how he used to look, said the woman from New Jersey very very quickly. He was beet red. And now he's not. And his skin was so bumpy. But now! See! See how flat his skin is! Her eyes came away from the wall to meet the astounded and uncomprehending glares of the family from Tupelo.

The worthless boyfriend mumbled something to the fat lady.

The woman from New Jersey peered at him. What did he say? she asked the grandmother.

He wants to know what happened to your kid, she said.

The woman from New Jersey screwed up her face in disbelief.

What? she said.

He wants to know what happened to your kid, the fat lady repeated.

What do you mean? said the woman with the brown hair, owl-eyed with rage. He was burned! Everyone in this hospital was burned! Your granddaughter was burned! She's going to look just . . . just like . . .

She searched the whole corridor for a word but there was none anywhere to end that thought with. And Carl was tugging at her skirt, wanting to go on.

Just you wait a minute, said the woman from New Jersey with the brown hair, pushing her son's hand away from her. Just wait a minute, she said. Everybody just wait. She put a strong hand on his shoulder and took a deep breath. I have to say something, she said to him.

She turned to face the family from Tupelo, but even her

anger could not force them to look at her. They still stared at her son.

You don't seem to realize what this boy has been through. She pushed her hair back off her face. He's been burned. He almost died. I mean, you haven't seen half of these kids here. Some of them don't even have noses. Some of them have lost their mouths. They're blind. And they can't hear. He looks very good. They can fix . . . they can do plastic surgery. He looks very very good. You just can't see it.

Her eyes were full of tears, she was so mad. This wasn't at all what she had intended to happen. But she couldn't drop it.

Your granddaughter's going to . . . she's going to be . . .

She bit her lip. She pushed her fingers into her eyes to try to make the tears go back. But it was no use. The people from Tupelo sat with their mouths open while she cried and Carl cried and the hot Galveston sun glared down with equal lack of sympathy on them all.

The woman from New Jersey finally composed herself somewhat, at least enough to take a long look at the ragged family from Tupelo, squinting at them through her tears as if they and not the sun outside caused the heat and the glare. She blinked again and again, but what she saw there was harder to bear than the hot sun ever would be. No longer the bloated grandmother or the pink slippers or the gray vacant faces of the lady's daughter and her daughter's worthless boyfriend, but now only the reflection of her son in their eyes.

Her stomach gave way, a deep dropping down of her bowels that opened to hunger and emptiness and caused her to tremble. She turned to look at her son, to look at what had so horrified them and was able, finally, to see him.

The left side of her boy's face was a flaming red. The skin there was hard and shiny and unnatural, wrinkled like the bottom of a riverbed when the water has dried up off it. His left eye was drawn down by the contracting of that skin nearly half an eyeball below his right. The left side of his lip was swollen up, frozen in an ugly sneer. That side of his head mocked the other, the right side perfect and freckled and unblemished, the left side having slid beneath it, like mud on the side of a mountain. Dull tufts of hair clung to his scalp. His ear was gone.

The woman from New Jersey slumped down in the chair she had occupied earlier in the afternoon. Oh God, she said.

Lord have mercy, said the lady from Tupelo.

Carl came and sat down next to his mother, tugging on her sleeve, but she was too stunned to move.

The worthless boyfriend lit up another cigarette, then leaned over and said something to the fat lady from Tupelo. She mumbled a reply and he answered and the fat lady's daughter acquiesced with a nod. The woman from New Jersey watched their conferring with only half her attention and waited to hear if it would mean anything to her.

The fat lady from Tupelo turned in her direction. He says you need something to cover yourself with, she said.

What? said the woman from New Jersey, dully. She studied them, trying to make out what it was they meant.

Yeah, said the fat lady. You can't go out there without something to cover you. Because it's going to be hot, she drawled. It's going to be hotter here than it ever was in New Jersey.

Although the woman from New Jersey could not make sense of what the Tupelo people thought she needed, she realized that the suggestion was made without malice of any kind.

I always cover myself, the fat lady went on. Keeps me from the sun.

There was a leaning forward of the fat lady's daughter, then a shuffling around with her hand on the floor. She brought up the ragged black taffeta umbrella. She handed it over her mother's stomach to the outstretched hand of the worthless boyfriend and then he, cigarette in mouth, eyes narrowed against the smoke, pushed it up its handle until it opened, limp and spokeless in places, but still serviceable. He passed it back to his girlfriend's mother and she took it and held it out toward the woman from New Jersey.

This'll cover you good, said the fat lady, almost tenderly. It'll cover both you and him.

The woman from New Jersey blinked. I can't take that from you, she said.

Well, you better, said the fat lady. We're the only ones here that got one.

The woman from New Jersey could not move. She could not even imagine touching the black umbrella that the fat lady in her own way held out so graciously toward her.

And the two of them would have hung suspended there a long time, held by the one's insistence to give and the other's inability to accept the gift, only the boy stepped forward finally and took the ragged covering from the Tupelo lady. Thank you, he said carefully.

He picked up his mask where it lay on his mother's lap and got the purse that sat beside the chair she had slumped into. He pulled at her hand to indicate that it was time they should set out and she obeyed, standing up and letting him lead her out and away from the narrow waiting corridor, away from the fat lady from Tupelo and her daughter and the daughter's worthless boyfriend. And then he brought her down to wait at the end of the hall in front of the elevator, even though he knew that she never took the elevator if she could help it.

Five in the Morning

J unior Ahrens had invited his friend Roy Wilkes over to
spend the night on a weekend just before school closed.
It was at the end of May with spring about to break headlong into summer and Junior Ahrens and Roy Wilkes were
both almost eleven years old. To set the record straight, Roy
was going to celebrate his birthday the next day, a fact that
caused his mother to balk at the idea of his going to Junior's
house overnight.

But I want to, fussed Roy.

It's your birthday in the morning, his mother said.

I already had my party, Ma, he reminded her. And all my
presents.

It was true. There had been a special cake for Roy at the
Hills' picnic the week before. And another cake for dinner on Wednesday. And presents at the picnic and several
more at their house. And checks from grandmas, which
had already been half-banked and half-spent. And the main
present, a basketball, already brought out long before time by

Roy's father because he hadn't been able to hold off teaching Roy how to play.

But we want to wish you a happy birthday, said Roy's mother. Haven't we always done that for everyone in the family? Isn't that what we always do for Sally and Bert? Fix you a big breakfast in the morning and sing you happy birthday? You can even watch an extra hour of cartoons.

But Roy thought he was too old to be interested in these family traditions. He just wanted to spend the night at Junior's house.

The matter of the overnight at Junior's was brought before Roy's father. He said that a person could do whatever he wanted on his birthday. It was the only day you could get away with it.

And so, on the eve of his eleventh birthday, Roy found himself sitting in Junior's kitchen. The back door was open to let the warm night air come in. Through the screen Roy and Junior could see Junior's older brother, Bud, and his friends sitting along the low back-yard wall, talking to some of the neighborhood girls. Roy and Junior watched these twilight shadows with little interest, for they had more important things to think about. Junior's mother had bought an enormous watermelon and she'd made a big jug of iced tea, and Roy and Junior set about enjoying these with determination.

Roy brought down some glasses from the kitchen cabinet and Junior put three teaspoonfuls of sugar in each. When the tea had been poured and the watermelon cut, the counter was thick with a sort of lacquer made of sugar and tea and watermelon juice, but none of this bothered Roy and Junior. They were content with the sweet savor of watermelon, which they dug out in spoonfuls from the heart of the fruit, and the wonderful sugared taste of the first iced tea of summer. Broken laughter came to them from the back wall where the night drew on soft and dark around Bud and his friends and their girlfriends, but Roy and Junior ate on steadily.

Well, asked Junior after some time had passed, did your Dad teach you how to play basketball?

Yeah, sort of, said Roy Wilkes, trying to swallow a big piece of watermelon.

What did he tell you?

I don't know, Roy said.

So how many baskets did you make? Junior persisted. He wiped his mouth off on the bottom of his T-shirt.

Roy shrugged his shoulders. He hadn't counted.

Ten? Twenty? said Junior.

But Roy was busy wiping his nose with the handkerchief his mother made him keep in his pocket. He didn't answer. Anyway, he had something on his mind about his birthday that he'd been trying to settle so he didn't much feel like talking about basketball.

I'm going to have to get up at five in the morning, he told Junior after a while.

Five in the morning! Junior said.

Well, said Roy. That's when I was born. That's what my mother and dad told me.

And that's what had been troubling him. Ever since his mother and father had told him about the day he was born, he felt somewhere inside himself that it was necessary for him to get up on his birthday at exactly five o'clock too, just like his mother had. He didn't know why.

His mother and father had been sitting together on the front porch one night last week after dinner. They sat in the big old porch chairs and talked that way they talked, a few words here and there, referring to things only they seemed to know about, laughing now and then. Roy had come out on the porch and sat down on the top step.

So our boy's growing up? he heard his father say to his mother.

Hmmmmmm, said his mother.

Roy looked up. His father and his mother were both looking at him.

You'll be how old? said his father, his tone of voice changing, talking now right to Roy.

Eleven, said Roy.

His mother sighed. I remember the day you were born, she said. Remember? she said to Roy's father.

Your mother had to wake up at five in the morning just to have you, said his father. And she kept kicking me.

I did not, said his mother.

Get up! Get up! his father continued. And then I had to get up and call Mrs. . . . what was her name?

Mrs. Fritz.

Mrs. Fritz.

Why did you call her? Roy wanted to know.

She was going to deliver you, said his mother.

You started being born so fast, said his father. Mrs. Fritz hardly got here before you came out.

But your cord was tied around your neck, said his mother. I was so scared. I thought maybe we'd have to get you to the hospital right away and it was so far away. But it turned out to be all right. You were all right.

Roy wanted to know then what a cord was and why it was tied around his neck and had the same thing happened to Bert and Sally?

No, that never happened with Bert and Sally. Only with you. Roy's mother laid her head back against the big chair she was sitting in.

That was such a nice time after you were born. That never happened to me before either. Mrs. Simmons from down the street came in to sit with me. She came and brought a chair and sat down right beside the bed. I was still awake but so tired and I lay there with you in my arms for hours, it seemed, without saying a word to Mrs. Simmons, without feeling like I had to say anything at all to her. And that has never ever happened to me before or since.

Hmmm, said Roy's father. Do you remember what else you did that day?

What?

When you started screaming?

I wasn't screaming, was I? Roy's mother frowned. I was just crying.

Roy's father thought for a minute. Well, he said. It sounded like screaming to me.

Roy's mother shut her eyes and after what seemed to Roy an awfully long time, she sighed deeply and looked directly at him. That was after Mrs. Simmons left, she said. It was late in the afternoon and I was aching so bad all over. I guess I was really tired. I remember that I was staring at you, holding you in my arms. You were perfectly formed and so peaceful and then it came to me just suddenly that the end of life, the very end of it, no matter what, is death and that I had given you life just so that you could die. I knew that I never wanted to do that again. Never wanted to have any more children ever again. And the thought of it made me so sad, that I began to cry.

Scream, said Roy's father.

They all three of them sat quiet for a long time after that, looking out over the immense starlit sky and thinking. After a while, Roy decided he would go in and get in bed, at least read in bed if he wasn't actually ready to fall asleep. He got up and kissed his parents good night.

Well, said his father. What do you think? His voice had that funny quality in it that Roy could never tell whether he was serious or joking.

Roy shrugged his shoulders and went inside, but he'd been thinking about it ever since, especially tonight. He told Junior the whole story, in as much detail as he could remember.

Ugh, said Junior. Your mother sure does scream a lot.

By this time, Roy and Junior had made their way up the stairs and into their pajamas.

You're really going to get up at five o'clock? asked Junior.

Junior Ahrens had a big clock that stood on his bureau with a sort of bell on top and he wound it up very officially and pulled out the button to set the third hand at exactly five. There, he said, turning its face deliberately in the direction of Roy's bed. Don't bother waking me up, he said. They both fell asleep minutes later.

But Roy didn't sleep very much that night. Junior had left a flashlight beside the alarm clock at Roy's request. Roy had gotten out of bed and clicked on the flashlight at ten minutes after two and then again at twenty-two minutes before four and once more at four-thirty. Then he began to feel really tired and was afraid he would fall back asleep if he lay down, so he brought the clock down beside him with the flashlight and sat on the end of the bed staring into the darkness, clicking the flashlight on and off every few minutes, dozing off and then starting up and dozing off again. But at exactly a minute before five o'clock, just before the alarm rang, he woke to his appointed hour.

Junior woke up at the sound of the clock too. The sight of his friend with his flashlight and his clock in such an intensity of waiting caused him to feel that waiting was also his own duty, so he went and sat down at the end of his own bed, hoping that whatever it was Roy was waiting for would happen fast so they could go back to sleep or drag their blankets downstairs in front of the TV and watch some cartoons.

From where they sat, they could look out the windows over the back yard, out into the sky, down over the city, and this they did, still dull and sleepy, letting the gray-blue morning and the last of the stars fill up their heads. The enormous maple tree in Junior's back yard had just put out new leaves and they rustled shyly against each other. Some birds sang. But the house was still, and Roy could only remember one or two times in his whole life when he'd been up that early.

This is when I was born, eleven years ago, he thought to himself. He began to rehearse the story of his birth over and over to himself, getting lost and forgetting now and then, picking it up in a new place, his mind, like the sky, hazy and full of the night still, thinking about his mother and her crying and Mrs. Simmons coming and his mother not talking to her and the lady his father called to come deliver him that he'd never even met and the cord that was tied around his neck, while Junior sat close at hand and studied him.

The sun began to ascend from over near the edge of the maple tree, so that the stars ceased to shine and the night was pushed aside. Even if Roy sat all day, he didn't think he would understand what it was his parents had told him, but he continued his faithful watch, waiting for he didn't know what.

Are you done yet? asked Junior when the clock said it was five-thirty. Roy shrugged his shoulders. He didn't know. And right then, he wished he'd spent that night at home.

88

My Sister Disappears

When I was nine and my sister Emily was thirteen, she had a date with Jimmy Gray and Ma was all excited. It was for the junior high prom and Jimmy Gray was the best-looking boy in the eighth grade. What's more, Emily liked Jimmy Gray. She liked Jimmy Gray even more than she liked Skylar Van Ness, who had also asked her, and whose family had money.

Plenty of it, Ma said.

My sister then was a beautiful girl with dark curly hair that set off her face like a little cap. She had a quick and engaging smile, a face wide and full of charming irregularities—freckles and dimples, eyes that looked at you but seemed at times to be about some other business—a slim beginning figure and strong legs that came from years of ballet dancing and gymnastics. My clearest memories of Emily are of her turning sure and steady back-flips across the green back yard of our growing up, and of this date, of her coming down the stairs in her white dress for the eighth grade prom.

Up until that time, Emily had been popular at school and a good student. At the PTA meetings, all of Emily's teachers complimented Ma on Emily's personality, on her beauty and her charm. The days went by for my mother in that time when Emily was thirteen in a sort of delirium of excitement and anticipation over all the things that Emily was doing: she had received the award for the Most Popular Girl in the eighth grade at Maplewood School, she was Miss Grissom's star piano student, she was the prima ballerina at Miss Natalie's School of Dance. There was no hint anywhere that this would not always be so.

But now suddenly, right during this time when Jimmy Gray asked her to the eighth grade prom, right when she turned thirteen and without any warning, something began to go on inside her that would change all of that.

Jimmy Gray was handsome and he was popular too, the most popular, and he was on the football team. Ever since he had asked Emily to the dance, Ma had been talking about how lovely Emily would be if she did something special and clever like the clever children we used to watch every Sunday on the Ted Mack Hour or the lovely girls whose talent Ma was so in awe of who skated in the Ice Capades in Radio City. Ma was certain that Emily would be the beauty of the prom if only Ma could have things the way *she* wanted them. She had been driving back and forth to town every day to pick up this or that to complement Emily's dress, which was white with a long pink satin bow. Ma found some rhinestone earrings and a rhinestone necklace and then some pink satin slippers, soft ballet slippers like the kind Emily wore to Miss Natalie's dance class, and Ma was certain these things would make Emily striking and unusual. The pink satin slippers would be different, not like the dyed pumps Ma knew every other girl would wear, and they would remind people that Emily was a ballerina.

But Emily, I remember, was not at first as concerned with what she was going to wear as she was with what exactly she would find to talk to Jimmy Gray about during the long evening that lay ahead. She and her best friend Jane Randolph spent the whole week before the prom writing down every word that Emily would say and every word, hopefully, that Jimmy Gray would say back.

Jane Randolph had red hair and always wore tartan skirts. She and Emily sat with their heads bent together at the old desk in the living room, pencil and tablet before them, and tried to make certain that there would be no lack of conversation.

Hello, Jimmy, read the first entry in their script. That was Emily talking.

Hello, Emily, Jimmy would say.

How are you? Emily would say next.

I am fine, Jimmy would reply. I had an interesting and exciting day playing football with my friends. I scored two touchdowns and we won the game against Maxson Junior High.

That is exactly what Jane Randolph and Emily hoped Jimmy would reply, for then it would open up the opportunity for Emily to say, Oh, that's nice.

Oh, that's nice, I heard my sister Emily say out loud, just for practice, but her voice was tentative and shy.

Jane Randolph was appalled. No, Emily, she told her, you will need to say, OHHHHHHHH, Jimmmmmmmmmy, how nice!!!! And Jane Randolph clutched her hands to her chest and wiggled in admiration, which made both girls laugh, but Emily didn't laugh very loud and right away she started worrying again.

Well, she said, twisting her hair around her finger, that will get us as far as the front door.

Ummm, said Jane. Why don't you say goodbye to your mother?

Goodbye, Ma, Emily wrote down carefully on the tablet of white paper.

Goodbye, Mrs. Field, said Jane Randolph. Write that down, she said. That's what Jimmy will say. Then he'll say, So nice of you to let me take Emily out.

So nice of you to let me take Emily out, Emily wrote down. She chewed on the end of her pencil and stared at the wall.

Now we're in the car, she said.

Oh, that's nothing, said Jane Randolph. You can just talk to his mother and father. Then they worked out five or ten minutes worth of the kind of things you talk to mothers and fathers about, like the weather and how nice it is, or if it's bad, how bad it is, and then school, how much you like it and your grades, if they are good, but Emily didn't want to talk about her grades because they weren't so good all of a sudden—she had trouble concentrating and they kept getting worse—so they decided to scratch that and talk about the latest recital at Miss Natalie's School of Dance.

By then we'll be at the school. We'll get out of the car. Now what do I say?

Then the two of them worked out all the possible things you could say while you were at a dance, like about the decorations and about where to hang your coat and how maybe a person could spend some time talking to the chaperones and everything you might be able to say when you actually had to stand close to each other and dance. It took the better part of that week, but from all that I heard, the two of them got Emily and Jimmy Gray into the dance, through the dance, out of the school, down to the Park Avenue Tea Room for a soda, and then back home.

Then he's walking you up the sidewalk to your door, I heard Jane Randolph say on the Thursday afternoon right before the Friday of the prom itself. And you say to him . . . Emily!

But Emily was staring off out the window of our living room to the roof of the Krantzes' house next door, a practice she would bring to perfection as the years took her away. Of course she wanted to go out on a date with Jimmy Gray. Wasn't that a triumph? And yet she was afraid and it wasn't just of not having anything to say. And it wasn't just of Jimmy Gray and the eighth grade prom.

Emily!

Huh?

Now you say, Thank you very much.

Thank you very much.

Write it down.

Okay.

Write down, I had a wonderful time.

I had a wonderful time.

Well, gee whiz, Emily, you need to sound real bubbly, the way Betsy Ahrens does. You know, Thannnnnks soooo much.

Like that? Emily frowned.

Sure. And then he'll say, I like you. I want you to go out with me again.

He will?

Yes, of course. And then he'll say good night.

Emily wrote down, Good night. Then what? she asked.

I don't know. He might try to kiss you.

Oh no. What should I say?

Jane Randolph stood up. Say, Ohhh baby! and put your arms around his neck. She bent over and threw her arms around Emily. Emily shrank away, but Jane Randolph kept on. Ohhh sweetheart, she whispered and shut her eyes and

93

made kissing noises. Kiss. Kiss. Kiss. And then Jane got real quiet and real serious.

Just don't let him touch you here, she said solemnly, touching herself on her flat chest.

Why would he touch me there?

I don't know. But if he does it will fizz you up.

How do you know?

Betsy Ahrens said so.

Oh. Jane sat back down and Emily took up her tablet of paper again. I won't let him kiss me, she said.

Well, then, he probably won't take you out again, said Jane Randolph.

But his mother and father will be down in the car, Emily protested. They'll be watching us.

Well, said Jane Randolph. I don't think they can see that far.

I remember that was how they talked about it. I listened to them all week, sitting on the front porch near the living room window pretending I was reading a book.

Finally Emily was so anxious from worrying about what she would say that on Thursday night she told Ma she couldn't go. But Ma had already spent twenty dollars on the white dress and fifteen more on the rhinestone earrings and necklace and the satin slippers and she wasn't about to let Emily turn down a date with a boy as popular as Jimmy Gray, so there was an argument. Emily was crying and crying and told Ma she didn't like the pink satin slippers Ma thought were so adorable and she didn't like the rhinestone earrings and necklace. Ma was mad. How come Emily hadn't said anything before? And what was the sense in going out anywhere when you would look just like any other girl? What was the sense in dyed pumps when every other girl there would be wearing them? Didn't Emily want to be different?

No! Emily yelled at Ma. I don't want to be different. And she said it with such force that Ma was struck dumb and the two of them stood there for a while without saying a thing.

How can I go anyhow? Emily finally said. I don't even know what to say.

Oh stop, Ma said abruptly. Of course you'll know what to say. Just say whatever comes to mind. Why, I've never been at a loss for something to say.

Emily wept bitterly and had to stay home from school on Friday morning, she felt so sick, and Ma finally relented and said she didn't have to wear the pink satin slippers, she could just wear the low white pumps she already had, and she didn't have to wear the rhinestones. But Ma was so put out that she stayed in bed that morning herself, the door to her bedroom shut. And there was nothing harder for any of us in those days than to see Ma do that. Even going to the prom with Jimmy Gray was not as hard as seeing Ma like that, so Emily said finally that she was all right and that she would go and that she would wear what Ma had planned so Ma got up out of her bed and set about the final preparations with determination.

While Emily was at school that afternoon, Ma laid the dress and the slippers and the necklace and the earrings out on Emily's bed and went downtown and bought a boutonniere for Jimmy Gray and a box of Helen Eliot's chocolates all wrapped up to give to his parents as a thank you gift for driving them.

Oh Ma, nobody does that, Emily wailed, and another argument began to brew so Ma pushed the chocolates to the back of the refrigerator and said they would wait and see how Emily felt about the chocolates later on.

At six Ma began to help Emily get dressed. Ma insisted that Emily wear deodorant and she had bought some, a roll-on. Ma rolled it up and down her own arm to show Emily how to use it and Emily, after much protesting, finally put some on.

Then they argued about Emily's hair which had come out of the pincurls Ma had insisted on just a little too curly and Emily wanted to wash it all out and she wanted Ma to just go away and leave her alone, when the doorbell rang and Jimmy Gray was there, at our front door, and the date itself was about to begin.

Dad answered the door and Ma rushed downstairs to greet Jimmy and then rushed back upstairs to get Emily to come down, leaving Jimmy Gray sitting in the yellow armchair across from Dad, who smiled pleasantly, but, like always, didn't say a word. Emily was still crying and it took Ma a few minutes to get her to stop and to get her face cleaned up, but finally she came down the stairs looking, even with Ma's pink slippers and rhinestones, startlingly beautiful.

She stood at the door of the living room and both Dad and Jimmy Gray stood up to acknowledge her beauty. Emily smiled shyly. The script that she and Jane Randolph had worked on so carefully all week was still upstairs on her bureau. She had had it all ready to stuff into her little pink satin purse, but Ma had seen it and insisted she leave it home and so Emily stood there trying to remember even the very first line, but you could see from the fear in her face that her mind was a blank.

Jimmy Gray was also speechless. Even though he'd probably imagined himself going out with Emily for at least the last two weeks, he seemed to have nothing whatsoever to say to her now, at this moment. Her dress and her bare shoulders startled him. She didn't look at all like the girl in short-sleeved sweaters and plaid skirts he'd been staring at this past year.

Dad and Ma walked Jimmy and Emily toward the door.

Dad went and got Emily's coat and helped her to put it on while Ma worked hard to keep the conversation going.

The two paused at the front door. What time should we come home? Jimmy Gray asked, his voice husky and then thin. It sounded a little like something he'd been practicing or that his mother had said he should ask.

Oh, don't worry, said Ma, just go on. Have a wonderful time.

Emily went out the door first and then waited awkwardly for Jimmy Gray to hold open the front porch screen for her and then waited again for him to walk down the steps with her. We watched them go down the front sidewalk, looking straight ahead, and then we watched them get into the car and pull away.

It was right around that time, during the summer after the prom and during the beginning of that next school year when she went to high school, that the Emily we knew disappeared and another Emily came to take her place. This new Emily got bad grades and put on weight. She was moved down to all the lowest-level classes and was afraid to go to school. She would leave the house in the morning when all the rest of us went off too, but she would only go as far as Park Avenue and then she would turn and come back home, lying on her bed all day with the covers pulled over her head.

Ma in terror took her to doctors and psychiatrists to have her evaluated, but they had no answers, had no idea where the Most Popular Girl at Maplewood School had gone to. They gave her tests and asked her many questions and they told Ma that this new girl was very slow, with a very low IQ, and that she would probably never get out of high school and would almost certainly never hold a job.

She began to see less of her friends until she had almost none. Jane Randolph got very popular and became more of an acquaintance than the best friend she had been. Jimmy Gray moved away to another state and wrote a card back at Christmas about a girl he had met who reminded him of Emily, and he said that this girl was his new girlfriend.

But it wasn't Jane's getting popular or Jimmy Gray's moving or even their date to the eighth grade prom that made Emily go away, though Ma for a long time tried to place the blame on each of these. Perhaps she shouldn't have forced Emily to go on that date. Maybe it had been too much for her.

But it wasn't anything Ma had done. And it wasn't their relationship, which from that time forward was difficult.

It wasn't anything at all that you could put your finger on, though Ma, even now, when she is eighty-three and Emily is nearly fifty, still studies where she can at last put the blame.

It was only that someone else had come to live where Emily once lived, a someone heavy and distracted, whose mind moved like lead, who could not remember, whose medium seemed to be no longer air, but water, and whose movements to displace that water took time and an enormous and visible effort. That person took up residence where Emily had been, pressing her slowly out and away, and though we hoped always, whether out of love or hatred or frustration, that the Emily we knew—that lithe and freckled ballerina, that astonishing beauty in the white prom dress— would return, she never has.

Am Entering Woods

It is June, the June of Dad's last summer.

Upstairs in their beds lie my father, Nathaniel Edward Field, my mother, Ada, my sister, Emily.

Ma is snoring, propped up in her bed against many pillows, her hair white, her nose long and thin.

Dad lies flat on his back, his body lean and bony, spare. His hands are folded over his chest, his eyes pressed tightly shut. He's only pretending to be asleep. Sleep comes dear this summer, refusing to enter him in the impenetrable darkness of those long close nights. It's fickle too, coming to him at the oddest hours—midmorning, just before supper— making him conspicuous, an object of Ma's attention.

Down the hall Emily lies stiff and anxious on her hard narrow bed, the sheet held tight over her head. She cannot sleep either, will not be able to really rest until that moment when Ma begins to insist that she must get up. Get up and help! Then the sleep comes heavily, like a sledgehammer, and is almost impossible to fight against.

*   *   *

The high-ceilinged kitchen in this house is old. Dirt has caked itself into every corner. The paper on the walls, once gay and whimsical, has come loose. My mother cannot see too well anymore and what she cannot see, she says, she doesn't care about. If it bothers you, she tells me when I come to visit, you clean it.

This house grows empty, this house once full. House of plans and schemes, house of lists, dreams, new wallpaper and paint, of my brother Jimmy in the hallway on the floor folding newspapers, of my sister Emily coming shy and lovely down the stairs in her white prom dress. It is dawn. The sun is up in the old kitchen, coming in the back door and in the windows, falling on the sills whose dust my mother cannot see and doesn't care about.

In this house my father rose early, dressed and took his breakfast, setting out down the back path toward the garage in his dark suit and business hat, his overcoat across his arm. At five he would return, coming up the path, through the kitchen, on up the stairs to the bedroom where his brown leather slippers waited for him beneath the chair at the foot of the bed.

He was an engineer. In this house, in the evening, before my mother called us in for supper, he sat in the green chair in the living room and read and took pleasure in dry, colorless books on bridges and air pollution, on sewage and asbestos shingles.

Tuesday nights after supper he drove downtown to the Fireman's Hall where the Hounds for Harmony held their weekly sing. Twice a year the Hounds put on a program in the high school auditorium and then, for the month or so in advance of it, he would be gone many nights, planning costumes and platforms, props and the order in which the various quartets and choruses would perform. Later they would honor him for his tireless contribution to the preservation of barbershop singing in America and Ma would fuss because the lawn went unmowed, if it was summer, or the sidewalks hadn't gotten shoveled, if it was winter, or in any season, because he wasn't home in time for dinner.

Weekends Dad rode a horse. When we were younger, he rode a friend's, but when we left—all but Emily—he bought his own horse. He named him Silent Man, after his own most disturbing trait. He stabled him in north Jersey and became an active member of a polo club there. At their annual banquets the members of that club praised Dad for the constant care he gave the fields and facilities, for the unfailing enthusiasm he displayed, for the patience he showed in working with the new and younger players, men about my brother's age. Ma complained that she was not comfortable among so many very wealthy people, that the horse was eating them out of house and home, and that Dad was never home on the weekends. And much later, when Jimmy himself had kids, he claimed that Dad, because of his horse and his barbershop singing, neglected us kids, didn't have time for us, never touched us or told us he loved us.

Novembers since I can remember Dad went to Maine, hunting deer and elk with a group of men just like himself. New England men. Plain and spare. Laconic. Unimpeachable. Dry and dull. At least us kids thought so.

He left early in the morning, long before we woke up. Long before those brittle silver dawns broke through the trees in the back yard, he headed out down Watchung Avenue toward Route 22, crossing up into Connecticut and Massachusetts by way of New York City, taking the coast toward New Hampshire, Portland and beyond—all in one day, reaching the woods before evening. The cabin where they met every winter was somewhere past that, beyond the last towns, beyond the last paved roads, deep in the woods beyond anything that the rest of us—Ma and us kids—understood.

We were never invited. It was a man's trip to start with, so that left Ma and Emily and me out. We would have been in the way and we would not have wanted to go anyway, having enough of Ma in us and then our own crazy New Jersey energy that the exaggerated silence and slowness of that crowd would have driven us nuts. We liked the shore much better. Lavellette and Seaside Heights. We liked lying around on the beach all day and walking the boardwalk at night, and if we were going to take a month to go anywhere, it would be to the shore in the summer and not to any cabin in the middle of nowhere in the dead of winter.

We saw it later, anyhow, in the spring, lying on our stomachs on the living room rug while Dad projected home movies against the window seat. A gray log cabin. White snow everywhere. On the ground. On the cabin. In the sky. Deer hanging by the front door suspended between poles. Dead. Ugh.

And then there were those men. Just like Dad. So slow to answer and so hard to stop once started. Walking around in plaid caps with earmuffs, attending with such seriousness to the business of camp.

Just as we'd suspected. There was nothing there to interest us.

But wait. There were parts of the movie that were a lot more interesting than that cabin. We made Dad go back and show us again. Look. Pictures that flew across the tiny screen. Look, Ma. Pictures of the woods themselves. Lines and lines of trees against thick heavy snow. Suddenly a man would appear. He would be trudging along in front of the dark rows of trees. And then, just as suddenly, he would disappear. Just the woods again. Then an arm would dart out from behind a tree, waving frantically, or a whole body would march towards us without a head. The woods again, black against white. Now what? A line of headless bodies without feet. But so merry, their arms beckoning to us, Come on. Come on in. Waving at us. Hello. Hello.

Dad laughed, but Ma complained that the film he bought was too expensive just to fool around with and that a man who couldn't take decent pictures ought not to have wasted his money on a movie camera.

But those were the pictures we remembered. As far as we were concerned that was the trip Dad took those Novembers. Not to the gray log cabin. Not to the place where the deer hung suspended between poles and the men went about their business wearing earmuffs. But to the woods. Those woods. Dark against light. Vast but familiar. Where men who were as long and as dull as a Sunday afternoon suddenly were not themselves.

Once he passed beyond that first line of trees there was no way for us to get word to him if we needed him or for him to talk to us should that unforeseen desire ever arise in him. The telephone lines ended where the woods began. He always stopped at a little store and bought a postcard, some winter scene. And mailed it to us. It would be delivered at home two days later, signaling that he had arrived safely at his point of departure and that the real trip was about to begin. The message was the same those seventeen years I lived at home, written in his careful hand, and as brief and oblique as he ever was: Am entering woods.

Dad doesn't eat much anymore. He doesn't dare tell Ma that he isn't hungry. His excuse is that what she fixes is either too hot or too cold. He keeps her banging around in the kitchen for hours trying to get it just right.

Emily doesn't eat at all, preferring a steady diet of coffee and cigarettes. Underneath the TV table in Ma's bedroom is a hat box full of vitamins the doctor recommended Emily take in order to stabilize her, make her able to get and keep a job, straighten her out, but Emily declares that the pills are big enough for a horse and there are too many of them and she finds ways to trick Ma into believing that she has taken her daily requirement.

Ma is always hungry, always hungry. She will buy a cake in the frozen food section of the supermarket where she often goes just to get away and eat it all at once, sitting in the car in the parking lot.

It is the summer of Dad's last year and the business of meals is, to say the least, taxing. It is hot, a year without rain. The New Jersey lawns are brown and everything irritates Ma: The meals. Dad. Emily. The running up and down the stairs. The going back and forth to town. The trips down to the doctor's and the endless bills from Sussman's Drug Store. Emily's determination to find another job and/or get married and/or have children. Dad's desire to sleep.

And he is leaving just the way he always left. Going down the path without looking back. Entering those woods this last time without so much as a postcard. Going finally where he cannot hear her complain about the houses at the shore that he should have bought for them but never did or about the horse and how expensive it is or about the subscription to the *New York Times* that costs them over a hundred dollars a year that he never reads. Just slipping off.

Do you want to talk about it? she asks him one day, meaning should they admit to themselves that there is something wrong, that he is dying, should they bring it out in the open and discuss it.

No, he says.

*   *   *

Emily's room faces east and is already flooded with early morning sun. It surrounds her, persistent and surly, hot already. She is pretending to sleep, anxious and afraid in herself of the confusion of such orderly things as the breakfast table waiting downstairs that Ma always sets the night before, the notes Ma writes that sit beside Emily's cup and saucer: TAKE THE NEWSPAPERS AND THE BOTTLES TO THE RECYCLING CENTER. THIS MUST BE DONE BY NOON. THEY CLOSE AT NOON.

Emily is between jobs. The last place she worked was in a nursing home down near the hospital. She worked there longer than she'd ever worked anywhere. Three, maybe four months.

The first month she worked at the nursing home she talked about the old people and how they loved her, how caring for them was really what her life was all about. But by the second month she was complaining, saying they were stupid and she was tired of them. Then she hated everyone there and Ma found out that she had been moved down from the wards to the basement where the laundry was and she was folding sheets. The head of the laundry didn't like the way Emily worked, said she was mindless and couldn't concentrate, and the colored people she worked with teased her, called her stupid and got her alone to taunt her about getting fired. You gonna lose your job, white girl.

Before the nursing home she worked in a restaurant as a bus girl, but she quit before they could let her go, and before that she was laid off from the A&P for not paying attention, and before that, before the time she drank the whiskey and ammonia and tried to drown herself, she worked in a dry cleaner's and as a secretary in a church and as a waitress and as a school bus driver.

Now she thinks she might like a job as a babysitter. She searches the paper every day for work. She has told Ma that she is going to take care of children and that she loves them and because Ma rages and will not allow her to do it even if she finds the work, Emily is set and determined that it will be so.

Sometimes Emily wears plaid blouses and striped pants together all in one outfit and underwear that has gone for long stretches unwashed. Unless Ma can get ahold of it. Unless Ma remembers. Sometimes Emily wears heavy black wool ski pants in summer. Sometimes she walks downtown with her pajamas under her raincoat. Sometimes, if she is lucky, she has money. Many times she is on an errand for Ma—to get stamps, for example—and Ma has called ahead to find out the exact price. And so Emily has only the exact price in her raincoat plus the extra for the cup of coffee she likes to have. Sometimes her hair is combed, but just as often it is flat on one side or the other and the same side of her face is red from having slept on it so long. Sometimes when she has nothing to do, when she is unemployed like she is now, she is all afternoon in a coffee shop called Grunings, on Fifth Street. She gets very sick there from too much coffee and too many cigarettes and has to get up and go to the bathroom so she can throw up.

Most times, though, she will spend the whole of her long days asleep on the couch in the living room and the whole of her longer nights just wandering. From her bed to the kitchen to the living room to her bed. Upstairs and down. Particularly this summer, when she has nothing much to do and Dad is dying.

Emily has a friend named Fred. Sometimes she meets him at Grunings in the afternoons. He is a widower, some twenty years her senior, who likes coffee and cigarettes as much if not more than she does. He is a union boss, an old carpenter. He reads the paper twice a day and catches the news on the TV early and late to see how his men will be affected.

He likes to explain things to Emily because he can see she's led a sheltered life and doesn't always have union people on her mind. He likes to tell her how messed up the country is and how unbalanced it is, especially out of the favor of unions, and he drives his talks at her with a vengeance, as if he were pounding her full of nails. His speeches are filled with emotion and scrambled further because he mutters and whispers against the possibility that Grunings is filled with informers, and she listens with a glazed, dogged look, her face screwed up tight so he will know she is trying to understand, watching the bitterness in his mouth and eyes.

When he is finished, she will hum for a while, a little embarrassed off-key tune she's been working over some twenty years, and when she is done with her humming, she'll often make a speech of her own, saying, I am just a simple girl, Freddie. I am just a simple girl. There are parts of me that are quite smart and there are parts of me that are not. I am telling you the truth so I won't fool you. I am not exactly stupid but I am simple and I am a good girl. Sometimes everything is clear and sometimes it is twisted up, and then she will rub her forehead to show that it is so.

And often this gesture will cause her to launch forth on the story of her own life, since that story in essence began with the same twisting in her head when she was thirteen. It is a story that has many embellishments and that once begun rushes on headlong and does not stop until she either forgets to talk or Fred gets up. It is a story that amazes her more each time she tells it, how it could possibly be that all these things happened to her. It puzzles her and causes Fred to say, You ain't got no confidence in yourself, Emily. It's your mother what done it. You need to get away from her.

Fred and Ma don't see eye to eye. In her body and soul, Ma is the summation of all the things that Fred hates. A Republican. A college graduate. An overseer of the English language. Anti-union. And Ma, though she appreciates his attention to Emily, holds him totally accountable for the fact that he says ain't and don't where isn't and doesn't are the only acceptable alternatives. She also begrudges him the dinners that he ate at our house nearly every night that spring, Emily insisting that it was the way it had to be. Since Dad barely ate and Emily only liked coffee and cigarettes, Ma was essentially shopping and planning and cooking for Fred and herself.

Where does he get off? she complained to her sister, our auntie. A grown man!

And Fred, for his part—though he didn't mind the considerable savings on groceries that those meals afforded him and though he felt he had to go and eat for Emily's sake, to protect her from any further damage by her mother—got tired of listening to Ma rant and rave, digging and pushing at him where she knew he was most vulnerable, always taking the side of Big Money, as he called it. He took the arguments personally, which was exactly how she meant them to be taken, though she always insisted she did it for argument's sake alone because she loved a good argument and forgot it as soon as it was over. But Fred's English she could not forget and did not forgive.

Fred and Emily have been seeing each other for nearly two years. Emily likes to pinch him on the cheeks and peck at him with her lips and even sometimes, just for effect, to kiss him full on the mouth. But not for long. She likes to brag about him and call him her Freddie. She likes to tell Ma that she and Fred are going to get married and have some kids and that she loves him. Deeply.

Go on, says Ma. You're too old to have kids and you wouldn't know what love is if it bit you. You don't love anyone but yourself. And if you're so crazy about him, why do you let him sit out there in the front of the house for hours waiting for you on a beautiful Sunday morning? Or forget about the dates he makes?

These kinds of questions don't have answers. There are Sunday mornings, in fact, when Fred will sit outside till noon because Emily is asleep and Ma and Dad are asleep and because Emily has forgotten that she and Fred had planned on getting started to the shore by seven. There are nights when he takes her to a play or to the Garden State Playhouse for a ballet or to hear Barbra Streisand sing and she hums the whole way down there in the car and then falls asleep in her chair right after the curtain rises. But Fred is infinitely patient. He's as patient as Dad—who is famous for his patience—ever was.

And whether she slept or whether she saw it, he will tell her what the play or ballet or singer meant as they drive back home, so then she can tell Ma and Ma will understand that you don't need to go to college to have culture.

Ma, whose attention has been caught by the light coming in the upstairs bedroom and pushing past the dark lilac-scented shadows, is startled, wakes up, remembers that tonight is the night that the Hounds for Harmony have decided to come over and surprise Dad with a serenade of his favorite tunes to cheer him up. There's beer and pretzels to be bought and an assortment of crackers and cheeses. Though Tony Leonetti when he called insisted that she not put herself out. They would only stay just for a while, he said. And there is food to get for supper. And the house to be straightened. And a thousand things to be done and they all somehow hinge on Emily's taking the newspapers and glass bottles down to the recycling center.

The button of Ma's pajamas is open over her immense stomach. She rolls forward and groans, arching herself upright, and sits there itching her head and staring at the floor, trying to get hold of her resolve of the late dark night before. She will not yell at Emily. Ever again. But just thinking about Emily causes Ma to jerk up, lumber around past Dad's bed and on down the hall.

Emily! she whispers loudly, pushing at that sleeping figure's shoulder. I have work for you to do that must be done now, she begins. And continues down a well-worn path that includes the necessity of Emily's helping out, her laziness, her silence, the state of her room, her addiction to cigarettes and coffee, the time she spends at Grunings every day, the whereabouts of the change from the money she gave Emily yesterday for the stamps, the need she ought to feel to get out and meet some people. And wends its way invariably back to work, how Emily cannot work as a babysitter, how, in fact, if she would only just help out at home and have a hobby like needlework like Molly Lacey's daughter has and would volunteer down at the hospital, she wouldn't need to work at all. They have plenty of money. There's no reason to work if she would just be content at home. God knows they could use the help. And she could make some friends through her volunteer work.

But the sight of her daughter, now well past forty, and all that her solid inert form bespeaks, causes Ma to break her resolve not to yell. She yanks Emily's hair and Emily, protesting loudly, escapes down the hall to the bathroom and locks herself in.

The sound of the tub filling up infuriates Ma even further.

If you get a job as a sitter, she hisses in toward the doorjamb, I will call them and tell them everything. EVERY-THING!

Dad is awake, but keeps his eyes shut, listening to this argument whose official stances he knows as intimately as he knows the deep pain in his backbone, as the insistent weight on his legs and arms.

You don't have to work, Ma is whispering to the bathroom door. We have plenty of money. If you'd just give me a hand, help with the meals and the dishes . . .

Dad waits for her tone to shift. He knows it will, as surely as the pain will increase the minute he tries to really go to sleep.

But you never help! You just won't be content.

Emily is deep in the tub, humming her tune, waiting for the story of her life to begin, waiting for it to pass by in her mind so she can catch a piece of it and lay it all out before Freddie, who not being right here, right in front of her, can't tell her she lacks confidence, can't blame Ma for all the things that have gone wrong. Stop! Here's the part about California, about the time she spent in San Francisco, about Vic.

Oh, Vic.

He told her he loved her. He asked her to be his fiancée. And doesn't asking someone to be your fiancée mean you want to marry them? Don't you think that's what he meant? Isn't being someone's fiancée worth giving them two thousand dollars?

I want you to take all the newspapers in the playroom and all the bottles on the back porch and get them down to the recycling center, Ma hisses. Make sure you ask for Mary. And no coffee! Drink your juice and eat your toast. It's already in the toaster. And don't . . .

Ma takes all her phone calls downstairs, except when Dad is downstairs and then, despite her arthritis, she takes them up in their bedroom. She whispers into the telephone. Does she tell everyone about him? Does everyone know that he doesn't want to eat anymore or that he sleeps most of the day or that he cannot stand the sight of the *New York Times* or *Business Week* or the sound of the Monahans laughing across the street? The phone calls go on just beyond his hearing. Everything is whispered, a secret. There is something happening that is very wrong and Ma will only whisper when she talks about it. And Jimmy and I when we call long distance are too cheery, far too solicitous.

This whispering and this cheeriness irritate him more than anything else. They join up with the pain in his back and the deep aching in his bones and make him what he has never been before: sharp and cranky. And the full weight of his irritation, needing an object, has fallen on Emily. He hurts too much to remember the lovely girl in the white formal coming down the stairs for her eighth grade prom, or the remarkable antics of her young and supple body as she leapt and turned across our back yard.

As far as he's concerned, she has always been what she is now. A person to be prodded and nagged. A middle-aged woman who seen too close has a mustache and tight painful wrinkles around her mouth, who stinks of cigarettes, whose touch is fierce and painful. He can only relax when she is not in the house. He has long since ceased to care whether she works or doesn't work, whether she helps or doesn't help, whether she is content or miserable. He just doesn't want her here while he is . . . sick.

The fight is on. But Ma decides that since Emily has locked the bathroom door, she should take advantage of this temporary setback and get dressed.

Ma is a big woman and pulling on her girdle takes some time. The stockings are no easy chore either. Her arthritis bothers her. And since she is growing blind, her dress—she discovers much later—is inside out and she has on one black shoe and one brown.

Emily knows exactly when Ma isn't standing at the bathroom door anymore, though Ma doesn't announce her departure.

Emily jumps up out of the tub and flies down the hall, putting on whatever she's thrown on her chair from the night before. She races downstairs. She bypasses the toast and the juice and the grapefruit and, fumbling with the whistling teapot, turns it on high to make some coffee quick before Ma comes down and catches her.

The newspapers are in stacks in the playroom. They are heavy and unwieldy and are best broken into manageable parcels. This is how we were raised. To plan. To think things through. To consider how we will do something before we begin. Although Ma as she gets older confesses that she never did anything except by jumping in headfirst.

To take these papers in big stacks is to take what Ma calls a lazy man's load. A lazy man's load is a load you think will take you only one trip. But you will be deceiving yourself. A lazy man's load is always unsteady. It is inevitable that you will fall or that you will drop it and then you will have to clean it up and then you will have to start out all over again. It will cost you more time than several trips with smaller loads would have taken. The only one who is being cheated is you.

But Emily is racing the clock. She has the lazy man's load lecture down by heart and she doesn't want to hear it again. If she moves fast enough, she'll escape Ma's telling it to her again. She'll do what she's always done. Move. Grab. Shut everything else down—her ears, her eyes, her mind, her heart—and get the thing done.

She picks up an enormous stack, blindly, without thinking and with no obvious effort. It is this uncanny strength of hers that finally got her moved down from the wards in the nursing home to the laundry room in the basement. The old people, the ones who were able to, complained that she hurt them when she picked them up and she picked them up just the same way she now picks up the newspapers. Quickly.

Just to get it done. Just putting her hands out and grabbing.

She lugs the stack out of the playroom, pressing the newspapers against the kitchen sink while she opens the back door, knocking over dishes stacked there, dirty dishes that haven't yet been rinsed for the dishwasher. She is down the steps, down the path, unmindful, leaning over to let the garage door up without even putting the newspapers down. But she has forgotten the keys to the car and can't get in the trunk. She leaves the bundle lying on the back of the car, on top of the trunk, and heads back up to the house where the teapot is whistling to wake the dead and makes her coffee, dumping milk and sugar in it to make it overflow the plastic cup's edges, humming that tune of hers for a little company. And lights a cigarette. And sits down at the table, even knowing that Ma will soon be down, may even now have her foot poised out over the top step, be fumbling with the banister, scratching her head.

It doesn't matter. Emily smokes and drinks, slurping loudly on the coffee, fishing around in her head for bits and pieces of her life story so she can catch a little of it, grab its tail, let it swim before her. She stares at the bricked kitchen wall, which once was white but has suffered the ravages of Ma's cleaning policy and is now yellow with stains, a perfect backdrop for any daydreaming that might come up.

Don't you smoke! There is a hissing from over the banister. Ma had just about finished getting her first stocking on when she smelled the cigarette. And has come to the railing in her bare feet. Don't you dare smoke. I'll have your head.

Yeah. Yeah, says Emily. And sets out down the back steps with a second bundle of newspapers. This one is an undisguised lazy man's load, loose ends trailing from its sides, the stack every which way in her arms. But she has forgotten the keys again. The second stack sits on top of the trunk with the first and is followed by a third and then a last.

She tries for another cigarette, but Ma is ever vigilant. And she knows exactly where Emily is in the task she has set her, because, as blind as she is, she has eyes for Emily that never dim. Though she can hardly see her hand in front of her face, she can see the nearly thirty yards from the second floor windows down to the garage and she has decided to post herself at the landing until the job is done.

Get the bottles now, she whispers loudly over the banister. They're on the back porch. And put out that cigarette.

The bottles are in paper grocery sacks on the back porch. Emily grabs them up by the top of the bag and wanders down toward the car, her eye and mind on California and the day that Vic called her his fiancée. Ma is signaling from the second floor window in a desperate pantomime but Emily isn't looking, isn't listening.

Pick them up from underneath! Ma even demonstrates for an imaginary classroom full of school kids sitting on the landing. But it is too late. One of the bags breaks open and the bottles smash down on the macadam driveway.

When Dad had the driveway put in, he had a square court lined out in white paint and put a backboard and basketball net up over the garage. My brother and his friends played basketball there while Emily and I sat on the grassy embankment of the back yard. Or we all stood in line to play kickball, the four corners the bases, the acre beyond where you dreamed the ball you kicked might go. Everybody came out to play in those days. Paul and David Ianello from Lake Street. The Kramer girls from next door. Vicky Griswald and Cynthia Morgan and Pam Troth and Betsy Stanich from the neighborhood. And Jimmy's very serious friend, The Rat.

And if it was summer, right around three o'clock, the Good-Humor man would come bumping down along Lake Street in his white truck, raising dust toward that spot across from the Crazy Man's house where he always parked. The whole bunch of us would head out to catch him, buy our popsicles while the Crazy Man rocked back and forth on his front porch, crying out, Mama, I'm going to die. Mama, I'm going to die. And stroll back home to a shady spot under- neath the trees in our back yard where we could stare out at the driveway and the acre beyond and prepare ourselves to play kickball until it got dark.

But the only thing going on now on the old macadam driveway is Emily's impending two-step with the devil who gets hold of her whenever she is trying to run away from Ma. He holds her tight so that she cannot think whether to go back to the house or to get down on her knees to pick up the glass or to get into the car or just to run far out among the trees in the back lot and hide. Ma is upstairs watching and fuming, giving Emily plenty of advice Emily cannot hear, raging because she knows how Emily in these situations is held and caught and that anything and everything probably can and will happen.

The other sack finally gives way too, breaking open, the bottles landing on the driveway, and Emily follows them, falling down on one knee in a small pile of broken glass. One by one she picks up the pieces of glass with her right hand and puts them into her left, exactly the way she used to play jacks and do the trick Cherries in the Basket, sweeping the jacks up from the floor by threes and fours before the ball hit the ground again. Only the pieces of glass are not obedient the way those jacks used to be. They don't stay in the basket at all. No sooner does one go in than a second falls out. No sooner does she go to reclaim that second than a third comes tumbling out of nowhere. And Emily could go on like this a long long time, the same way she used to play jacks all of a summer afternoon, except that Ma has made her way down to the back porch and is yelling.

Emily!

Emily starts up, surprised and terrified, her knee bleeding from the glass. She heads for the garage. She's going to do something, either start the car or open the trunk, but—God forbid—she still doesn't have the keys. And getting them means going up past Ma, means having to deal with Ma, means having to explain herself. So, assuming a sort of air of knowing what she's doing, she makes her way up the back path, humming that tune of hers, this time for consolation and encouragement. She keeps her eye on the door behind Ma and puts a kind of hard look on her face, one calculated to give the impression that she's not fooling around. And comes right up against Ma who is yelling and sputtering and saying, Emily, why didn't you hold the sacks on the bottom and why don't you eat your breakfast and why do you light up a cigarette when I've told you a million times not to and why don't you just be content staying at home and why don't you ever just help and why don't you ever use your head and what in God's name happened to your knee?

I need to get the keys, Emily yells right at Ma, just so certainly. Isn't it obvious that she has to have the keys? But to complicate matters, she can't find them, not anywhere, not in her purse or up on her bureau or in any of her coat pockets or sweaters, and no matter how fast she moves, Ma is behind her, following her everywhere and going over some history that Emily would rather not remember.

But finally there are the keys, right in her purse where she looked the first time. She grabs them and goes down and opens the trunk. But it's heavy and so she forces it and it's only when the newspapers shift and slide onto the garage floor that she realizes why the trunk wouldn't come up.

She moves quickly now, throwing the papers by small sections into the back of the car. Scooping the sacks of bottles up in her arms, she throws them in, gets in the car and pulls out, hearing the tires crunch over the glass she didn't get up. And accelerates quickly, going out of the yard as fast as she can. Without her purse. Without her breakfast. Without having brushed her teeth or combed her hair. Just moving as fast as she can to get as far away from Ma as possible.

The glass ordeal came to Dad only as a series of signals. Ma's heavy footsteps on the stairs. A time without sound while she waited at the landing where the windows looked out over the yard. A rapping on the window. More footsteps. Ma yelling. And then the car squealing in the yard. All it meant was that Emily was gone and he could finally rest.

Ma stares out the jalousie windows of the back door. She leans her head against the wood frame, stares at the floor, and sighs.

It's all her fault.

She has no one to blame but herself.

She never should have taken that pill the doctor gave her during Emily's delivery.

So what if she screamed and cried out for relief?

That doctor should have known better than to give her a pill that might hurt the baby.

She knew what Jimmy and I always said when she started talking like that. Oh, Ma, it wasn't any pill that made Emily like she is.

Damn kids!

What did they know?

And Dad never any help at all.

And Auntie and her brother Arthur both telling her she treats Emily like a child.

Like a child!

They ought to come try to live with her for a week.

And the kids always saying, You shouldn't support her, Ma. Let her out on her own to make her own way.

Make her own way!

Did they see what kind of way she'd make?

Gives two thousand dollars away to a man she's known for two days.

And keeps talking about marrying him, and that whole incident now over fifteen years old.

Swallows whiskey and ammonia while she lives by herself in Woodbridge.

Can't keep a job. Can't take orders.

They don't know what they're talking about.

Or don't want to know.

She starts back upstairs, pulling herself along by the banister, step by step.

If only Dad had bought those two houses at the shore like she told him he should have.

Then Emily could live in one house.

And Ma and Dad could live in another.

The three of them wouldn't have to live together.

And if Dad . . .

Then Emily could be close.

But not too close.

And Emily wouldn't have to work.

She could just be content.

Ma reaches the second floor landing, breathing hard. And stares out at the yard and the driveway and the back acre, a view she has studied now some thirty-five years. The hedge between our house and the Blacks' next door is full and green and the rosebush beside the garage is blooming.

And Godfrey. The lawn needs mowing.

She groans, starts back up the stairs.

Who will mow it?

Dad won't hardly eat, let alone mow.

And Emily? She can't be trusted.

And herself? She's blind. And her arthritis.

*   *   *

Nate, Nate, she whispers.

Dad is lying on his back, straight up, his mouth open in a profound sleep that he is not about to let be interrupted.

Nate! They must have some routine. They can't just keep going on like this, sleeping half the day away, with no particular thing to do. He can't just go on sleeping. Even if he doesn't want to read or watch TV, he must get up for meals. Even if he doesn't want to eat.

Nate! She shakes his bony shoulder.

He opens his eyes. He doesn't recognize Ma.

Go away, he says to Ma. The kids need to take the test.

What test? says Ma. She leans down closer to him, looking carefully at his face. What are you talking about?

He shuts his eyes tight.

Nate. Wake up, Nate. You're having a dream.

Ma sits down on the side of the bed. He feels her weight. He hears her sigh. Godfrey, she says. You must have been having a dream.

But he doesn't answer, lies there angry.

Ma gets up. Staggers slightly and steadies herself. Scratches her head and stands there studying the floor.

Doesn't this just take the cake? she says out loud, shaking her head back and forth, not caring whether Dad hears her or not. He's getting as crazy as Emily.

Ma is back down on the landing, stunned, held there by what Dad has just done. Something is wrong with him. With his head. He was doing a lot more than just dreaming.

She can't get it straightened out. Why was he talking about a test?

She sits down on the window seat, shoulders rounded, scratching her head. She is in that posture of defeat and despair that used to send us flying out the back door. She stays that way. Ten, fifteen, maybe twenty minutes, then gets up, fumbling along the banister for a hold, her foot, the one in the black shoe, poised at the top of the step. And descends.

She goes to the old desk in the living room and telephones our Auntie, who is spending her summer in Massachusetts with Uncle George because Florida, their winter home, is too hot.

Margaret, she says. She keeps her voice low. This is Ada.

How are you, dear? asks Auntie.

Weary, says Ma.

Is there something wrong?

Between Nate and Emily, I don't know what I'm going to do. And there ensues a long detailed description of Dad's and Emily's latest failings.

After the phone call to Auntie, Ma goes to the kitchen. There's a little pad of paper on the counter beneath the big window that looks over toward the Blacks' house and on that pad Ma begins to sort out the things she will need to buy at the store.

Beer. That's for the barbershoppers, even though Tony insisted that she get nothing. But you can't have nothing, any more than you can ask someone to spend the night and not provide them with clean sheets and a pillow. She has no idea how much beer to buy, however, since she's never had so much as a drop of liquor—ever—in her life. Her father drank enough to satisfy the thirsts of a thousand men.

She'll ask the man at the liquor store how much a man will drink in an evening if he only says he's going to stay an hour but will probably stay two. She can multiply that number times the number of Hounds that will more than likely show up, so she can figure it out, get it exact so that there won't be any beer left over, not a single can, in case Emily gets it into her head to consume what remains.

Pretzels.

Crackers.

Cheese. Maybe she'll just order a tray of small sandwiches from the Pickwick. So much expense. And for what? She wishes the Hounds weren't coming at all.

And what about dinner? She shuffles across the floor and goes into the kitchen closet and then back out to stand staring into the refrigerator and then the freezer. There are two Stouffer's Lobster Newburgs in there, which is one of Dad's favorites, but if she wants Emily to eat she'll have to buy a third frozen dinner and she has already had frozen dinners just last week and probably ought to have fresh corn from the market up on Second Street because it's summer and it's in season and if she has corn she'll have to get lettuce for a salad and some radishes and tomatoes and then she ought to serve steak with it. Except she always burns the steak, and she'll be nervous anyway because of the Hounds coming, so she should get those frozen dinners. That would be the best thing. Except if Dad notices that this meal is a recent repeat and refuses to eat it on that account.

She puts the pencil down and rips the paper off the pad. She'll decide when she gets to the store, like she always does. And if it's simple to get to Second Street today, she'll get the corn and if it's not, they'll have frozen dinners.

One last notation. For herself. *Ice cream.*

And another. *Sara Lee Bavarian cake.*

While she is thus ruminating on who will eat what and how she will manage to get to the different places she needs to get to without staying away so long that Dad will worry, Dad himself appears in the doorway between the kitchen and the dining room, fully clothed like he hasn't been in months. He is even wearing his hat, but Ma is stunned to notice that he has grown so thin, the hat appears to be floating on his head.

Why have you got your clothes on, Nate? she wants to know. Where do you think you're going?

We're going to go to the doctor's.

What do you mean? What are you talking about? We were just there two weeks ago. Has something changed? Don't you feel well? Are you upset with me? Godfrey, Nate, I didn't know you were having a dream.

I am fine, Mother. I want you to call down to Dr. Skenk's office and have him and his partner and the doctor from the hospital and that specialist meet us there. I want to talk to them.

You can't get four doctors together like that! Ma protests. They have other things to do. It will cost a fortune. And what do you want to talk to them about anyway?

There are things they should be doing that they have neglected.

What things?

I'll tell them when we get there, he says. And then, instead of trying to get past her, he goes back out the door and around through the dining room and the hallway and in through the other kitchen door to sit in the chair by the radiator, waiting—so it seems—for Ma to go upstairs and get ready so she can drive him down to Dr. Skenk's.

The doctor has made time for Dad and Ma to come in just after one-thirty, and has assured Ma that it is all right for Mr. Field to be feeling this way at this time. Though he can't promise that anyone besides himself will be there. Though he'll call the others and ask. Ma has insisted that Dad have breakfast while they are waiting to drive down to the doctor's and has stood by the sink while he eats, bringing him each course to make certain that he at least tries. Dad for his part has requested that she bring in the *New York Times* and he props it up on a silver stand in front of his place mat to provide a sort of screen and a distraction. But the news, once a matter of deep interest, doesn't interest him any more at all.

First there is Instant Maypo cereal, which she has cooked exactly like she has done for the past seven months in a row. One cup of water, a half a cup of Maypo, a teaspoon of salt. But Dad won't eat it because he says it has no salt and then Ma sprinkles a little salt on it and Dad says it is too salty and then Ma says to put some sugar on it and Dad does but by that time it is too cold and he doesn't want it. So she brings him the grapefruit out of the fridge but that hurts his teeth because, he says, it ought to be served at room temperature, even though he has never eaten grapefruit at room temperature since he's been married. So she makes him a piece of whole wheat toast with lots of butter, but he will only nibble at it.

He is antsy. He wants to know why Dr. Skenk has made them wait until one-thirty when—if he was taking care of his business properly—they should be able to come right away. It is a sign to him that the doctors are avoiding him, the same way they have avoided his case. Just taken his money but not done the work.

It's barely eleven o'clock. There are two hours before it's time to go and he can't go upstairs again and lie down because if he did then he'd have to put his pajamas back on and if he puts his pajamas back on, it would take more energy than he feels he has right now to get into his street clothes again and go down to the doctor's. So he wanders uncertainly in the hallway, not sure whether sitting on the couch in the living room or the chaise lounge on the front porch will attract less attention to himself. He decides on the chaise, because it is summer and hot and even a man who is well, even a man as robust and noisy as Jim Monahan across the street, would—in such hot weather—sit on his porch and read the paper.

But he is really tired now and has only just enough steam left to get to the chaise and fall into it. Oh, but there's a little chill and he needs a better pillow. The stiff back of the chaise makes his own back ache.

Ada! He calls out to Ma and asks for his thin white blanket, which is upstairs. She lumbers up the stairs to get it. And stops to make a phone call to Tony Leonetti telling him of Dad's latest whim and suggesting that maybe the Hounds should just forget coming tonight. And assumes that Tony will understand and drop the whole affair. But Tony pauses just a little too long.

What's the problem? Ma wants to know.

Well, I was just thinking, Mrs. Field, he tells her, that the boys were planning to come over already and getting hold of all of them at work—because there had to be at least forty who had planned to show up—would be hard and he was also just thinking that maybe in the light of this recent request of Nate's it might be a good thing for them to come ahead and cheer him up.

And Ma is just getting ready to tell Tony that she thinks that it will have the opposite effect, and to mention to him— rather remind him of—all the trouble that she and Emily had getting Dad to go down to the last barbershop concert at the high school because he was afraid the men would feel sorry for him, when she hears what she thinks is Dad calling out her name again and has to just give in and say goodbye. She goes back downstairs.

Where's the pillow? Dad wants to know.

You didn't ask for the pillow! She goes back upstairs to get the pillow. And considers a second phone call to Auntie just because she needs to talk to someone but she remembers that Dad is waiting. And after that there's another trip into the kitchen for the *New York Times* so he can have something on his lap should anyone come in and discover him lying down in the middle of the day.

He sleeps the better part of the two hours and could sleep another two only Ma is there shaking him and reminding him that he had wanted to see the doctor.

She drives them down in the direction of the hospital. Dr. Skenk's office is nearby. She can just barely see. Things are not clear anymore. She drives from memory.

Mother, warns Dad, there's a boy on a bicycle.

Tell him to get out of the way, she says, or there'll be one less boy.

Dad and Ma sit in chairs in front of Dr. Skenk's desk in his small, elegantly dark office. His partner is there, Dr. Lathrop, but the other two doctors, he explains, were not able to come. One is in surgery and the other is out of town.

What is he doing? Dad asks in disbelief.

I believe he has taken his family on vacation, Mr. Field, says Dr. Skenk.

The color rises from Dad's neck. We are paying him good money, he says. He is supposed to be at work on my case. Is he spending all my money on a vacation when he should be here?

I understand how you feel, Mr. Field, says Dr. Skenk, but Dr. Howell had planned his vacation months ago.

Dr. Skenk sits up a little straighter in his chair and tries a new approach. Your decision to come was made so suddenly. Don't you think we can talk things over between you and me and Dr. Lathrop and Mrs. Field?

Dad's head wobbles just imperceptibly. His lips, like thin lines drawn crookedly across his face, grow white.

I do not think what I have to say will have as much impact

as it would were the other two physicians here, he begins. Their not coming is just another demonstration of the point I wish to make. That being that the four of you are making so little progress in this case because you are not working together. You are not talking to each other. And because you are not talking to each other, you are each treating this case in a different manner. And nothing is being done. Nothing at all is happening. The case has not changed at all.

What do you think we should be doing, Mr. Field? Dr. Skenk asks.

That is your business, Dad raises his voice. That is your business. Not mine.

This speech has depleted Dad's resources completely. Dr. Skenk offers a gentle rebuttal, talking quietly about the difficulty of such cases and of the prominence of each doctor in his field. But Dad is so exhausted that he is barely able to listen and doesn't even notice when Dr. Skenk finally asks Ma if she will step outside the office for a minute.

Doesn't he understand, Mrs. Field? Dr. Skenk asks Ma. They are standing outside his office door.

Understand what? says Ma sharply.

That it's cancer. Bone marrow cancer. That there is nothing we can do. That he's dying.

Ma hardly misses a beat. She knows Dad has cancer. She has just never heard his diagnosis quite so bluntly put. But we are not a people to be caught off guard in anything.

Yes, of course, she says, of course he understands. He just wanted to talk. That's all.

And then, just for a second, she allows herself to be thrown off.

Are you sure? she asks.

They set out for home, but without notice Dad wants a shave and insists upon being driven up to Front Street to the barber's. She lets him out in front of the barbershop and circles around, down Watchung and behind the barbershop, to the public parking lot. And who is racing across the lot but Dad. She pulls up beside him.

What are you doing, Nate?

You were taking off without me, he sputters at her. You were going to leave me, he insists and will not be dissuaded. The only thing to do is to get his mind back on the shave, to get him going toward the barbershop. But bad luck! The shop is closed.

Why didn't you call ahead? Dad raises his voice to her.

You just this minute decided you wanted a shave, Nate, she says. And the barber has no phone anyhow. You know that. But Dad has forgotten about this idiosyncrasy of the barber's and all the way home he talks about Communists and how a man without a phone must be trying to hide something, must be dishonest, must be Red.

Now it is Ma's turn to be exhausted. She sits down in the big green reclining chair the first minute she can after she has him settled back upstairs in bed and sleeps a heavy sleep, forgetting Tony Leonetti and the Hounds and their impending surprise almost until it is too late.

Emily is back from the recycling center. Mary Stanich was there—Betsy and Ann Stanich's mother, our neighbors all these thirty-five years. Mary was full of pressing questions, about how Dad was and where Emily was working and how the rest of us were, where we were living and what we were doing and how many kids we had and what kind of kids they were. Emily answered all of her questions in a loud and hysterical voice, caught with an enormous armful of papers and all sorts of answers flooding into her head that had nothing to do with the right ones. She listened with her face all pinched up while Mary answered back to each answer.

About how Dad was so good and such a saint and always willing to help. And how Jimmy had been so smart. And how I had turned out surprisingly well for all the strange things I had done in high school and college. And how Ma was such a card.

Then Emily barked out a question about Betsy and Ann. Mary said that Betsy was a concert pianist and that Ann was in England and was married and had three children and halfway through that recital Emily stopped listening, though she kept nodding her head and breathing loudly and saying, Yeah, yeah, every few seconds. Yeah, yeah.

She had barely been at the recycling center for forty minutes. Yet the whole adventure wore her out. She wandered down along Front Street for a while and then she stopped in at Grunings for some coffee and stayed there a long time, going back over the conversation she had had with Mary Stanich standing on the loading platform at the recycling center. She took out the answers she had given and filled in answers that made her seem like a real person with a real life of her own. And when she had finished, Mary Stanich said that it was Emily who had done well and was married and had three kids and was good and was a saint. Emily was so lost in that acting out that she barely noticed that she was sick from too much coffee and cigarettes and had to slip off her stool quickly and make for the bathroom so she could throw up. After that she had a seventh and an eighth cup and some more cigarettes. And then, having nothing more to do, she headed home.

Ma is asleep in the green reclining chair and Dad is asleep in his bed when Emily comes in and Emily is glad, because the fewer witnesses she has to her difficulties, the better. She would not want it known right then, right at that very minute, that she has eaten nothing all day, has drunk ten cups of coffee—all on money she had to borrow from the girl who worked behind the counter at Grunings—and smoked a pack of cigarettes, has thrown up twice, once in Grunings and once on the way home, and has nothing—absolutely nothing—to do. It is not her whole life that stretches out before her but just the next hour, just this night to come and the fear that she will have to live through it.

She lies down on the couch in the living room and covers herself with an old quilt.

The phone rings at three-thirty. Ma is startled out of her heavy sleep, scratches her head, pulls herself groaning up out of the green chair. It is Artie Dove, inquiring about the Hounds' hour of arrival that evening and apologizing profusely for having waked Mrs. Field up, which it is obvious he has done, because she cannot orient herself, does not remember for several minutes that the Hounds are coming at all that evening. And when she does, she is panicked because there is still so much to do and so little time to do it in. She tells Artie, like she had told Tony Leonetti earlier in the day, that Mr. Field has not been himself today. She explains the episode with the doctors and Mr. Field's insistence on challenging them. But Artie, she sees, is as thick as most men are and understands only the greater need for them to come and cheer Nate up and to stick to the original plans at any cost because changing them will be more trouble than keeping them.

We'll see you at seven-thirty then, Mrs. Field, says Artie cheerfully.

She groans, climbing the stairs, thinking of all that lies ahead. She goes to the bathroom, then checks in on Dad to see that he is still asleep and heads off downtown.

She is back by five-thirty, honking all the way down the driveway from Pine Street, the car loaded with all that is necessary for a night's entertainment. Emily responds to the car's horn as if she were a machine and the horn the key that turned her on, waking up out of a stupor to stand dully on the back porch, waiting for Ma's insistent voice to set her fully in motion. Ma has also engaged the help of three black boys who come over every afternoon from Lake Street to play on the macadam basketball court—have, in fact, been coming over ever since we grew up and left the house. Maybe not the same three boys. But three or four or five boys who do not know us at all, our names or who we are or what we do or how our lives are lived out in that house, but who use the old basketball court because, I guess, basketball courts should not on any account lie fallow. They understand that it is part of the territory that when the old lady comes honking into the yard, they're to carry up whatever she has in her car and to listen to whatever she has to say without answering back.

And here they come, bringing up the cases of beer and the sacks of groceries, with Emily humming and stumbling along in between them. And Ma is orchestrating everything.

I did not know there was this much beer in all the world, she is saying.

And then, I don't care if you play in the yard all day if you want to, but when I come into the yard, you're to help me. That's the way it is.

And then, standing on the first step of the back porch to catch her breath and scratching her head: Seventy-five dollars. That's what I spent, she says, addressing no one in particular. The basketball players stare at her as if she were a statue.

All that for just one night's entertainment, she tells them as they pass her going back out into the yard. And I'll bet you Dad doesn't give a tinker's damn if they come or if they go.

*　　*　　*

Then the fun begins. Ma tells Emily in no uncertain terms to help. She is to help and to do it right and not to make any mistakes. She is to hurry up because the Hounds will be here at seven-thirty. She is to put the beer in the fridge so it will be cold. She is to put the crackers on plates. She is to put the chips in the green bowl under the sink. And the pretzels in the baskets in the closet in the playroom. And to take the trays from the Pickwick and put them on top of the beer that she has already put in the fridge.

Emily stares at Ma, her head cocked to one side, her eyes wide and unblinking. Ma fusses and complains as she shuffles along between the closet and the table and the fridge.

Here I've spent seventy-five dollars. For what? He won't come down. I don't have anyone to help me. You're no help to me. None whatsoever.

Yeah, says Emily. Okay. Yeah, yeah. She puts the crackers in the fridge. She puts a bag of chips in beside them. She remembers the beer and brings it over in front of the fridge and begins to tear open the cardboard around each six-pack. But the space she had thought might be there for the beer has already been taken by the crackers and the bag of chips. She holds the cans of beer out toward the shelves but nothing clicks. Nothing seems to offer any remedy. The crackers won't move. The chips seem too fragile to be touched. The beer sits at her feet and waits to be chilled.

And I will not have you smoking while the men are here, Ma is saying. The word "smoking" triggers a spurt of energy in Emily. She shoves the cans of beer into the fridge willy-nilly, some here and some there, some on top of the chips, some lined up conspicuously on the door in between the many bottles of salad dressing Ma keeps buying and forgets she has.

Okay, Ma, says Emily, when every can is in the fridge.

Ma comes up behind her. Godfrey mighty, what are you doing? She pushes Emily out of the way to try to rescue the crackers and the chips from the weight of the beer cans.

She puts a box of crackers in Emily's hands. Now put those on a plate. Emily heads for the cabinet where the everyday dishes are stored. No! Not those plates! Not plastic! This is company! The good plates! In the playroom!

The crackers in her hand make Emily hungry. She almost gets a handful of them in her mouth when Ma, ever vigilant, yells out, Don't eat them! Not a one!

Then there is the question of the green bowl and it is under the sink, just like Ma says, but it is dirty from disuse, a fact Emily doesn't notice. She shakes the bags of chips into the bowl, catching Ma's attention, and Ma remembers the bowl hasn't been used in years and wonders why in God's name Emily hasn't taken the time to wash it out. Then the chips must be picked out carefully, the bowl washed under Ma's watchful supervision, and the chips replaced without Emily's consuming a single one.

Finally the chips and the crackers and the pretzels and the trays and the beer are all in their proper places. Ma is banging the pots and pans around in preparation for supper the way she has done now lo these many years so that we all know that though we are sitting and resting and waiting for our suppers, she is not. She groans and complains as she bangs things around, imploring someone to take note of the eating habits of those she has to live with and describing the same. How Dad won't eat. How everything is either too cold or too hot for him. How Emily will only smoke cigarettes and drink coffee. Just to steady herself during this rehearsal she eats cracker after cracker from the plate that Emily has prepared.

Seeing that Ma is occupied, Emily drifts slowly out of the kitchen and settles herself back on the green couch in the living room so that she can have some time to think about her life, something she hasn't done since early this afternoon at Grunings.

She lights a cigarette and taking a long drag, she begins to dream. Her face twists and pinches itself up tight. She stares out the living room window at the shingles on the roof of Herm and Carol Krantz's house next door and to those shingles she, plaintively and with much strong emotion, pours out—once more—the story of her life.

I am just a simple girl. There are parts of me that are quite smart and there are parts of me that are not. I am telling you the truth so I won't fool you. I am not exactly stupid but I am simple and I am a good girl. Sometimes everything is clear and sometimes it is twisted up . . .

Tonight she is telling the shingles about Vic. He is there in her mind, as omnipresent as God, and God, she knows, is punishing her because . . . well . . . for two things: (1) that she did not sleep with Vic, and (2) that she ruined his life. Can God forgive her for all the bad things she has done? More important, can Vic forgive her? And will he come back and get her if he does?

Ah, here he comes now, drifting into her mind and into Malone's twenty-four-hour drugstore.

It's San Francisco and Emily is twenty-three. It's early in the morning, a Saturday, barely five A.M. She is sitting at the counter in Malone's drugstore. He sits down next to her and he looks at her, carefully at first and then with a great deal of intensity. On the green couch in the living room back home and nearly twenty years later, she watches this man watch her and knows that this is what he sees: a pretty girl, a good girl, a nice girl, not like other girls—a cap of black curls, strong legs, a good figure. She has never slept with any man. Nor will she, until true love comes along. She's on her own, has her own apartment, a job, and two thousand dollars in the bank.

She can smell him: that smell like Dad's closet, a man's smell, of sweat . . . and too, a smell of cigarettes, and something else, incense maybe. She can feel him looking at her. And the first thing he says—Couldn't you sleep last night?— makes her stomach tense with surprise.

She looks at him quickly. He is wearing a dark brown corduroy jacket with patches on the elbows. And he says to her again: Couldn't you sleep last night? He says it quietly, breathing out a long sigh on the first drag of his cigarette and watching her as intimately as if he were her lover.

No, says Emily. She looks at him again. His hair is curly. Black. She can't look in his eyes.

You're not from here, are you? he says.

No one has ever talked to her as if they knew all there was to know about her. No one has ever talked to her like this, in a voice this tender.

How do you know? she asks.

You're not like the girls from around here, he says. He has eyebrows that are long and mournful. He has beautiful brown eyes and he looks directly into her face. His hair touches the collar of his jacket and Emily wonders what Ma will think of him.

He has been watching her for weeks, he tells her. He is a teller at the Wells Fargo Bank where she has her savings account, but she probably never noticed him when she went in there. He knows where she lives and he has been wanting to get to know her. He thinks she is pretty and the sort of person he'd like to know.

He has told his friend Al, who works at the bank too and who lives one floor above Emily in her apartment building, to keep his eye on Emily until he, Vic, can work up the courage to introduce himself to her.

I don't know anyone named Al, says Emily. And I've never seen you before.

Emily runs her fingers over the old green couch in the living room and wonders, like she has many times before, if that had been the wrong thing to say. If she had not said that, maybe she wouldn't have said and done other things and then she would not be here, sitting on the green couch in the house she was born in, but would be instead in a home of her own with Vic.

Vic is still talking. He has been walking all over town this morning because he couldn't sleep and he's been feeling, well, feeling kind of lost, thinking about Emily and how he would like to get to know her, when he sees her sitting at the counter at Malone's and something in the way she is sitting makes him know that she didn't sleep last night either and so he decides that, even if Emily tells him to get lost, he will come in and sit next to her.

But he says, If you think it is wrong for me to talk to you, I will go away.

In Emily's dreaming, Vic says this over and over again. If you think it is wrong for me to talk to you, I will go away.

If Ma would give Emily the chance, Emily would tell her what Vic said—*If you think it is wrong for me to talk to you, I will go away*—many more times than she has already told her, to prove to Ma what Emily knows to be the truth, that Vic is a good man. Ma's voice interrupts Emily's dream insistently: Why would a good man be watching you for weeks unless he was up to no good?

She tells him now—she says it out loud, right in Ma's face—like she told him then, You may stay.

His name is Vic Ochoa. He is twenty-five. He was born in Los Angeles, the oldest of eight kids, but his father left his mother and she had to raise them on her own. When Vic was only ten, he had to start working, doing odd jobs for local grocery stores, loading trucks, peddling newspapers on the corner. And every cent he made then, and every cent he makes now except for what it costs him to live, he sends to his mother to help her with the family. At least, this is what he tells Emily.

Sometimes he had to go to school with holes in his shoes and without any breakfast.

To Emily, Vic Ochoa is as exotic as an angel. She has never met anyone so poor before in her whole life.

Vic has so many dreams. He is telling her: A man has to strike out on his own. Take myself, for instance. I'm pretty good with my hands. In fact, I think I'm real good. He holds his hands out in front of her so she can see them.

He wants to start his own home repair business. He has it all mapped out. At first he will be the only one working. But people will see that he does a good job and that he is honest and then his business will increase. Then he can hire another man and another and then another and soon he will be at the head of a whole company. He'll be his own boss.

Of course, dreams take money, he says. Guess a poor boy like me will be waiting on that dream a long time.

He watches her intently. Then says: You know, Emily, a man has to find some way to provide for his wife.

I thought you said you weren't married, says Emily.

He shrugs his shoulders, then takes hold of a piece of her hair and winds it carefully around his finger. I might be soon, though, he says.

Now Emily and Vic are in her apartment building. It is Saturday afternoon, just hours after they first met. Vic asks if he can come to Emily's room and talk to her some more. Emily doesn't think this is right.

This is a crucial moment, she knows. She knew it then

and she knows it now and Vic senses her hesitation: if she doesn't agree to have him come up to her room, he might never come back to see her.

Her room is just a bed and an old flowered armchair with its skirt half-torn and a little bench with dirty clothes on it sitting in front of an empty dressing table and a bureau. She is embarrassed that she hasn't done much with it. She sees it through his eyes, a dark room without personality, no trimmings, no light feminine touches. She even has her suitcase on the floor halfway under the bed with clothes coming every which way out of it because she has never yet unpacked, not for the whole year she's been here. The bed isn't made. It worried her then and it worried her later: would a nice bright room have made the difference?

She stands helplessly at the entrance to the room, paralyzed. She doesn't know where to sit. If she sits on the bed, he might sit near her. And then what? If she sits in the flowered armchair, he might sit on the bed and then he might do something suggestive. If she sits on the bench, then he would sit in the armchair and their knees would almost be touching. Where is the best place to sit? She can't move.

Vic helps her. He takes hold of her hand and shuts the door and leads her over to the bed. He sits on the edge and pulls her down to sit next to him, but when she does, she is very stiff. What's the matter, he asks her?

I've been a Presbyterian all my life, she tells him.

Yeah, he says. He rubs her hand with his thumb. Why did you say that?

I'm a good girl, she answers.

He leans in close toward her cheek, but she stands up quickly.

He is surprised. I thought you liked me, he said.

I do like you.

Why won't you let me kiss you?

I can't. I don't do that. I just met you.

He puts his head in his hands and shakes it slowly back and forth. Then he looks up at Emily. I just can't believe this, he tells her. You're different than any girl I've ever met.

He stands up. He puts his hand on her face and looks at her for a long time. I've just never met anyone like you before, he says. And do you know what?

Emily shakes her head.

I think I'm in love with you.

They meet again in the coffee shop later that day, and he tells her more about the business that he wants to start. It is a dream that is so close, just within his grasp. He just needs some way to get started. It is the only way he is going to provide for his wife.

They spend the evening and way into the night walking the streets of San Francisco and talking. She has never talked to anyone that much before; nor has anyone talked to her like Vic has.

That night Emily began to dream and to make her plans. He loved her. That meant that she would be the wife he kept talking about. He had said he loved her. That's what that meant. She believed in him. She knew that he could do anything he set out to do. But all he lacked was money. And she had money. She had that two thousand dollars. He could use that to start the business and then they could be married and she would be the secretary in his business.

It is Sunday morning. She is at Malone's counter and has not been able to sleep from thinking about Vic, from thinking about the wedding—it will just be a small one, no more than a hundred people to the reception. Her dress will be white and her bridesmaids will wear pale orange and . . . Gayle, the girl who works behind Malone's counter, wants to know how long Emily has known Vic.

Emily tells Gayle that she and Vic are in love and that it is true love and will last forever. Gayle frowns. Well, how long have you known him? she says again.

For at least a year, Emily lies.

Didn't you just talk to him for the first time yesterday? Gayle says.

Vic is the most wonderful and sincere person I've ever met, says Emily.

Look, says Gayle. I'm warning you: he's a con. He'll take every cent you've got.

Godfrey, Emily. Ma is forever coming into Emily's dreams. This man is a thief. Can't you see that?

I'm sorry, sister, says Dad, but this fellow was just playing with you. Dad is here in Emily's apartment, come all the way from New Jersey to bring her home. The moon has been forcing its way in through her window and threatening to get Emily, and, Emily says, she feels she can move the stars just by shifting her eyes. But even so, she doesn't want to leave the apartment because Vic might be coming back any day to get her. Dad keeps putting things into her suitcase, slowly and methodically. He's already bought her plane ticket.

Vic is back beside her. She has told him how much she loves him and told him how important it is for her to give him this money because it will help him to become the man he wants to be and to lead his own life. She has told him that she will marry only once in her life and that will be for true love. His eyes look right into her heart, those long mournful eyebrows. He takes the money.

He says that he has to go deposit it in the bank right away and leaves.

The next day, early in the afternoon, a man comes to her apartment. He is wearing a gray suit and a hat just like Dad's.

Do you know a Mr. Vic Ochoa? he asks Emily.

Yes.

Your name?

Emily Field.

And you are his . . . fiancée?

Emily's stomach leaps. Yes.

Mr. Ochoa deposited a rather large sum of money this morning in our bank. I am just verifying its source.

Yes, Emily tells the man in the gray suit. I gave it to him. I'm his fiancée.

She goes downstairs to Malone's at five o'clock, waiting for him to come see her after he is done at the bank, but he never shows. At ten she starts to walk the streets, looking for him.

The next day at Malone's, Gayle asks Emily if she has given Vic any money.

A little bit, Emily confesses.

Well, don't expect to see it again. Or him.

Ed, Malone's manager, comes up behind her. Listen, hon, he says, I hope you didn't get in too deep with this guy. He's a real con.

I tried to warn her, Gayle tells him.

Emily leaves right after her next cup of coffee. They can't be telling the truth. And she refuses to go back to Malone's. She doesn't want to hear Vic slandered like that. The days pass but there's no sign of Vic and when she goes by the Wells Fargo bank where he said he worked, he's not there.

She has no money left and she's not sure if she'll be able to keep the job she has, she's so distracted all the time. She needs that money back, but more than that, she needs to see Vic and get married and have him with her, so she won't have to listen to the voices of Gayle and Ed at Malone's. But he doesn't come back. For just a half hour, she succumbs to the voices in her head who keep telling her that Vic is a con; she has never listened to them before, but because of her fear of Ma and what she will do when she finds out about the money, Emily is tempted. So she writes a letter to the manager, Mr. Pyle, at the Wells Fargo bank and she tells him everything, that a Mr. Vic Ochoa has left town and he has taken her money and does Mr. Pyle know where he is and when he'll return. But when Mr. Pyle replies, the news is devastating and unexpected: the bank had let Mr. Vic Ochoa go a week ago because he had been suspected of taking money, although no one could prove it. But Mr. Pyle had not trusted him from the start.

But it doesn't matter what Mr. Pyle says about Vic, or that Vic possibly may have been a thief. It only matters that Emily was tempted to slander the man she loved, a man who called her his fiancée, and she is convinced that he has been let go, not because he was suspected of taking money, but because of her letter. She has ruined his life and he will never forgive her. She is afraid then, as she has been many times before, that she will ruin whatever she sets her hand to, so she stays in her apartment so she will not ruin the city of San Francisco, but it is hard, because the moon keeps coming in her window to get her and she can make the whole universe shift just by shifting her eyes. And it is there finally that Dad comes to get her and bring her back home.

For all these years, these questions have perplexed her:

If someone tells you he loves you, doesn't it mean he will marry you?

If someone calls you his fiancée, doesn't it mean he will marry you?

If you give someone two thousand dollars, doesn't it mean he will marry you?

She has been writing Vic letters, but not sending them, since she left San Francisco—in her mind, on paper, telling him where he can find work and that she defended him against the lies that people heaped against him. And she has been going over and over the time she spent with Vic and thinking through those questions intensely, daily, over and over again, and they all add up to one thing: Vic intended to marry her. But he changed his mind because (1) she didn't sleep with him and (2) she ruined his life.

Tonight they will eat out on the porch. No matter if Dad says he's tired and tries to get Ma to feed him upstairs. No matter if he doesn't want to come down. She and Emily will carry him down, if need be. Though she knows better. Knows that she would kill herself on the stairs trying to balance him and that he would not let Emily touch him. But the porch is the easiest place to feed him and it will get him down out of his bed, at least, so that when the Hounds show up—though how they are planning to surprise him she cannot imagine— he will be downstairs. And that is important, she feels, in light of the strange things he has done this day. Who knows what he might do with forty or fifty of his friends on the front porch and seventy-five dollars worth of beer and food in the fridge?

It's six o'clock. Their plates are warming up in the oven and strangely enough, on such a tight schedule, Ma has decided on steak and fresh corn and string beans and a green salad made up in individual bowls with some hot crescent rolls on the side. The water for the corn boils furiously, steaming up the kitchen.

Outside it is summer in New Jersey, hot, and even for a summer without much rain, sticky and humid. The afternoon sun is just beginning to give way to shadow.

Then everything is ready. The steaks are cooked and being held on top of the stove. The beans are buttered and salted. But Godfrey! The rolls are burning! And time—a relentless devil—dances across the old kitchen floor talking to Ma and giving her plenty to worry about.

Six-twenty and he's not even downstairs yet.

And who knows if he's asleep or awake or if he'll come at all.

Emily!

Emily is on the green couch, explaining to Ma—again!—that she would not let Vic touch her but gave him the money because she loved him and he loved her and she was his fiancée.

EMILY!

Yeah, says Emily finally. She sighs and uncrosses her leg. Yeah, yeah, she says.

I have to do everything myself, says Ma when Emily arrives. Your father won't get out of his bed. He's afraid of his own shadow. And you are just as bad. You're afraid to get work and you only get the most ridiculous jobs when you do try.

What do you want me to do? says Emily, suddenly and cheerfully.

What do I want you to do? says Ma, turning on her. I want you to be here to help me. I want you to stop daydreaming. I want you to stop sitting on the couch and smoking. I want you to get a job and keep it, no matter how tough it gets. Or stay home and be content.

Okay, Ma. Okay. Emily's body tightens in a habitual posture evoked by Ma's driving anger. Her arms stiffen. Her hands stretch out helplessly in front of her while she watches Ma shuffle round and round the kitchen. Muttering. Sighing. Complaining.

I can't see a thing.

The pans don't have handles.

Everything will get cold.

Your father won't eat.

I have to do everything myself.

And then suddenly—a break in Ma's tune!

Go upstairs and call your father! Tell him dinner is ready.

*   *   *

But Dad will not come.

He says he has to go to the bathroom, Emily reports back to Ma.

Ma is already on the stairs. What do you mean, he won't come? Of course he'll come. He has to come. The Hounds will be here in less than an hour. Seventy-five dollars worth of beer and food in the fridge! He'll stay in bed over my dead body.

She stops at the landing, breathing hard. She misses the banister and stumbles and then corrects herself and starts on up the last four stairs.

Nate, she calls out quietly. Her voice is careful and reasonable. Cheerful even. There is a small thin response from the bathroom. She stands outside the door. Nate, she says, dinner is ready.

He knows it is, he says. But he has to go to the bathroom.

She goes over to the digital clock between her bed and his and bends down to look at it closely. Six-thirty. Dinner must be eaten and the table cleared by the time the men start coming up the street.

Are you done? she says, standing back at the bathroom door.

No.

Are you sure? Sometimes there's that pressure on your bladder and you don't really have to go.

Yes.

Well, could you hurry just a little? I have everything ready.

I'm doing the best I can, Mother.

Ma sits down on the edge of Dad's bed and stares at the floor. She covers her eyes and shakes her head back and forth.

Emily has come to the top of the stairs. She stands looking pensively at Ma.

What do you want? Ma hisses at her.

Huh?

Go on back downstairs and watch the food.

Emily stares at Ma a long time, her head cocked, a little crooked smile on her face.

Ma, she says after a while.

What?

There's a job in the paper for a babysitter.

It's a quarter to seven and Ma has finally got all three of them out onto the front porch and sitting down at the dinner table. It's a small table, every inch of it covered now with the necessities of front porch dining and the requirements of the large meals that Ma insists on serving. Two bowls of vegetables. A basket of rolls. The old lazy susan in from the kitchen with all its accoutrements. There is even a little wobbly TV tray table that holds a bucket of ice and the jar of instant sweetened tea that is Ma's favorite brand.

Ma is tense, steeled against many eventualities. One is the phone. If the phone rings and it's one of the barbershoppers, she will have to get Emily's attention before Emily stands up and answers it and yells out information that would give the surprise away and cause Dad to go upstairs and refuse to come down.

A second possibility is that Dad might tell her that the food is cold. She will not listen. Or that he has to go back upstairs to the bathroom. She will not let him. He doesn't have to go.

Emily is shoveling food into her mouth quickly, barely cutting her steak, barely chewing.

Emily! says Ma.

Dad is staring at Emily, too. She is slathering roll after roll with butter and pushing them into her mouth.

There's no need for you to eat that fast, Sister, he says.

Listen to your father, says Ma. Now!

Yeah, yeah, says Emily. And then suddenly, defiant, as if she just woke up. I'm hungry, she says. I can eat any way I want.

You cannot, however, eat like that, says Dad. That's not eating. That is making a pig of yourself.

Emily stands up, although in a slightly awkward way. She had her legs crossed under the table and didn't bother to un-cross them before she makes her move to get away. She gets herself straightened out and heads in toward the kitchen.

Where are you going? Ma demands.

Nowhere, says Emily. I'm just going to get some tea.

The tea is here, says Ma.

But Emily is gone.

Nate, says Ma. She sighs. You shouldn't talk to her that way. She has feelings.

But Dad doesn't answer. And Emily is back. She has brought an ashtray and her cigarettes and a book of matches. She settles back in her chair, folding one leg underneath her.

You're not going to smoke, says Ma.

Why not? says Emily, lighting her cigarette. This is the porch, there's plenty of air here. I'm not bothering anyone. I'm a grown woman. I can do anything I want, Ma.

You are bothering us, says Ma. We are eating. And you haven't finished your dinner anyway. I want you to eat every-thing on your plate.

I ate as much as I'm going to eat, says Emily. And now I'm going to have a cigarette.

And this sort of conversation could go on all night, except that the phone rings.

I'll get it, says Emily and is up and out of her chair in a flash, leaving the cigarette to burn on the edge of her plate. She goes in through the front door and into the living room to the desk where the phone is. Ma can see her through the window that separates the porch and the living room.

Ma is struggling to push away from the table in order to

intercept Emily and the possible consequences of what she will say and do, but Emily has already picked up the phone and is yelling in that slow, surprised voice of hers, Ohhhhh. Yeah. Jim Monahan? Well . . . Why are you calling?

Godfrey! says Ma, struggling to get out of her chair. She is trying to get Emily's attention through the window. Jim Monahan is a Hound who lives across the street.

What time should you come tonight? yells Emily. Come where? she says. Oh! Oh! Oh! Over here?

But Emily's conversation on the phone doesn't have all that much impact on Dad. His attention has been arrested by a car that has pulled up on the corner of Pine Street and Watchung, not in front of our house but two doors down. It has caught his eye because someone he knows has a souped-up aqua and white Chevy like that. A man gets out of the car wearing bermuda shorts and a white short-sleeved shirt. His hair is the color of carrots. It looks like Artie Dove.

It is Artie Dove!

Mother, says Dad. Mother, there's Artie Dove on the corner.

So what? says Ma, trying to appear nonchalant. Maybe he's here for a visit. Nevertheless, she finally gets herself up out of the chair and knocks on the window at Emily.

Get off the phone! she says. Get out here and help me. Hurry! Hurry!

Dad is standing up.

Where are you going, Nate?

I have to go to the bathroom.

What do you mean, you have to go to the bathroom? You just went to the bathroom.

But he is already making his shaky way back up the stairs. Emily is still yelling into the telephone. Artie Dove is standing on the corner of Watchung and Pine, smiling and waving as other Hounds assemble there in preparation for the big surprise. Ma scrambles for the dishes, her mind whirling. She must get the table cleared and Emily off the phone and herself upstairs before Dad has a chance to lock himself in the bathroom. But this old body of hers won't move that fast anymore. Forks drop from the plates stacked too many and too awkwardly. She knocks over a half-glass of water and makes a long puddle on the top of the summer table. When she gets to the kitchen, it is overwhelmingly cluttered and from the front porch when she shuffles back that way, she can still hear Emily on the phone and she can see the group of Hounds swelling in size and noise as they prepare to approach the house.

Emily! she yells. Hurry! Hurry!

Ma stands at the bathroom door.

Nate?

There's no answer.

Now, Nate, she says, I had nothing to do with planning this. Nothing at all. Tony Leonetti called and insisted that they all come over and sing for you.

No answer.

They thought it might cheer you up. What's the problem? Don't tell me you're afraid?

No answer.

Are you afraid?

Nothing.

These are men you've known for thirty years, Nate. How could you possibly be afraid of them? Nate? . . . Nate!?

They don't need to see me, he says finally.

What do you mean by that? They don't need to see you. That's why they came. To see you. I bought seventy-five dollars worth of beer and food just so they could see you.

I'm too tired tonight to see them.

How could you be tired? Godfrey mighty, you slept late

this morning. You slept after breakfast. You slept when we got home from town. How much sleep do you need?

No answer.

Suddenly Ma can hear Emily's wild piercing voice down below yelling, Hello, Hello. How are you fellas doing? she is screaming out. There are the lower voices of the men punctuated with Emily's attempts at hospitality. Ma knows from experience that all forty men must be standing on the steps and spilling out down the sidewalk, trying to figure out what to do next, while Emily stands extemporizing at the screen door and doesn't have enough sense to let them in.

What shall I tell them? Ma says to the bathroom door.

No answer.

I'm going to go on downstairs then and tell them that you won't be coming down at all. They are going to be terribly disappointed.

They've been looking forward to this for weeks, says Ma. She scratches her head. I suppose I'll just have to entertain them myself. She sighs loudly.

It makes me sick that you're too frightened to come down, she says.

The Hounds at the door have taken to talking among themselves since Nate's daughter seems uncertain as to what she should do. It seems a little odd. Mrs. Field is probably up helping Nate get dressed. Poor guy. What a grand old fellow. Always willing to help. Always ready to give a hand. Selfless. Generous. Too bad about this cancer. Wonder if he's lost much weight. Didn't look too good last time he was out to see the show, much paler than usual. But the old gang here will do him good. Yes, indeed.

Now this daughter of his is a little difficult. She's had some trouble in the past. May be a little crazy. Wonder whether we should just go ahead and barge on in . . .

They look up. Mrs. Field is at the top of the stairs, her hand on the banister, her foot poised above the top step. A big woman. Always had something to say about everything. As much unlike Nate as a woman could be. Hard to understand how the two of them have gotten along all these years.

She descends slowly, not looking at them, holding onto the banister.

Wonder where Nate is.

Ma pauses in the hall. She looks toward the kitchen, her head still down, then turns and approaches them slowly, with great weariness.

Hello, she says. Tony. Artie. Jim. All of you. She looks out over the whole group without smiling. There is such a strange look on her face. It causes Artie Dove to turn and look backward, wondering if perhaps someone out on the sidewalk has offended.

Well, she says, setting forth in preparation for a speech of sorts. That wasn't much of a surprise, all of you standing out there on the corner like that.

Suddenly they are awkward, not middle-aged men but young boys whose mother has reason to be upset with them.

Certainly they had meant well. Though maybe they were a little noisy. But geez, they were glad to see each other. Hell, where's Nate?

A shifting occurs in the whole body of singers. Several cough. Others look away, back toward the corner, or down at their feet.

Well, says Artie Dove, we weren't as organized as we thought we might be, Mrs. Field. In fact, they had hardly been organized at all. Only just told each other to meet at Nate's around seven-thirty.

Yes, says Mrs. Field. She faces them all directly, accusing. I think you've frightened him off. I don't think he's coming down for this surprise of yours.

But, then—just when things could easily have become unbearable, when those who had meant to do good were about to be made to understand that they had done a terrible thing—there is a movement, a shuffling, at the top of the stairs. They look up and there they see him.

Look!

It's Nate!

There he is!

Why, here he comes!

Look, here he is, Mrs. Field! Hey, he hasn't changed a bit!

He is cautious about coming down. As he draws closer, they see that's not quite true. He has changed. He has that same quirky—almost cherubic—smile. But oh! he's pale. And very thin. And he's embarrassed, shy.

But Nate was always shy.

No, not Nate. He was quiet. He was reserved. But he wasn't shy. Not like this.

Yeah. Emily's voice breaks through the stillness that accompanies Dad's slow progress down the stairs. Here he is, she croaks out. Here's the guy you've been looking for, she repeats. She looks at him and then is caught, mesmerized. Her face screws up tight, just to study him.

Here he is. Here he is, says Ma. Now she's the one who's surprised.

The older barbershoppers are surprised, too, caught off guard by the change in their friend. But the younger men, the ones in their late forties—and there are even some very new men who are barely entering their twenties—who haven't been singing with Dad all these many years, are not affected so strongly when they see him.

One of them, Bill Cole, a man whose hair is brown and still intact, whose knees aren't knobby and whose legs are not blotched with varicose veins, steps forward to speak while the rest shift and relax and lean forward eagerly to hear what he will say.

How are ya, Nate? says Bill Cole, extending his hand. Geez, we've missed you.

Dad shakes Bill's hand.

I am fine, Dad says, very slowly and deliberately, the way he always spoke. He lets go of Bill's hand and holds his own hand, palm upward, toward Ma.

Ada, he says, is taking very good care of me.

Oh yes, says Ma, suddenly gay. Though he longs to be back in the hospital.

Dad smiles his quirky smile and turns to the Hounds to explain. Ada is referring to the great number of nurses I had surrounding me while I was there, he says.

Five at a time, says Ma.

Several of the Hounds on the steps let out whistles.

Yeah, says Emily.

They were very attentive, says Dad.

And young, says Ma.

Yeah, says Emily.

Oh, boy! says Artie Dove.

The Hounds laugh nervously.

Dad stands smiling expectantly out over the group of men.

Jim Monahan clears his throat. We thought maybe we would do a little singing tonight, Nate.

Yeah, Nate, chimes in Bill Cole quickly. What do you think?

That would be fine, says Dad.

But Ma can't stand all this deliberation anymore. Come on in then, she says. Come on inside the porch, all of you. And as they begin to come in the screen door and move awkwardly up along the porch, she says, There aren't enough chairs. But I already told you that before you came. Now who wants beer?

Oh no, say some. Don't trouble yourself, Mrs. Field.

What do you mean, don't trouble yourself? I have seventy-five dollars worth of beer and food in the fridge. You better trouble yourself. Godfrey, what do you want me to do? Polish it all off myself?

While Ma is fretting about the affairs of hospitality, the Hounds are assembling and reassembling around Dad, trying to figure out where to stand or lean or sit—if anywhere. Actually, they are wondering how they can possibly squeeze onto the porch and talk to Dad, instead of just staring at him.

Artie Dove moves over next to Dad and tries to get things rolling. We've missed you, Nate, he says heartily.

Dominic, one of the younger men, a handsome, skinny fellow with his hair slicked back and a wave over his forehead, says, Yeah, Nate, there was no one there to oversee the last show. You know—to make sure we were doing it right.

I am certain that Artie did a good job, says Dad.

Well, he did all right, Nate, but it wasn't like having you do it.

What does Artie have to say about all this? asks Dad.

Oh, it's true, Nate, says Artie. He crouches down next to Dad's chair and the effort makes his face go red and bleed into his carrot-colored hair. I couldn't get anything right. You're the only one who knows how to get things done.

Man, Artie is always forgetting things, says Joe, Dominic's friend. Right, Artie?

The Hounds laugh, joyful at the chance to make fun of Artie Dove.

Yeah, like the reservations he forgot to make at the Park Hotel for the Buffalo Bills, yells out Chick Grote. They were already here before he remembered.

Already sitting in the lobby of the hotel! echoes Dominic.

My god, Nate! Artie slaps himself on the forehead. Where were you when I needed you?

Lucky for Artie, they still had rooms available, says Chick.

Yeah, lucky me. But we very nearly had to throw a young couple right in the clutches of marriage out of the honeymoon suite just to get them a place.

The Hounds giggle.

Did the Buffalo Bills realize you forgot to make their reservations? asks Dad.

No, no, no, Nate, says Artie, standing up straight and blushing. Oh no, Nate, they didn't notice a hair out of place.

Catcalls and whoops.

But subdued somewhat, for here is Ma again with Bill Cole and Tony Leonetti and one younger man in tow, bringing trays of beers and insisting that everyone take a can and bring it on into the living room, where there is much more room and many more couches and places to sit.

We can just sit on the rug, Mrs. Field, Artie Dove tells her.

But no, Ma will not hear of it. Everyone must have a seat.

Emily! Ma yells at her from across the living room. Run over next door and ask Herm if they have some chairs to lend us.

Emily looks mystified.

The Hounds offer to help.

No, no, says Ma. Go on, Emily. She raises her eyebrows and Emily is off.

Some of the Hounds have squeezed onto both couches as tightly as they can, five to each couch, holding their beer cans carefully in their hands. One has taken the wing chair and three more have filled up the window seat while Ma has Dad sitting in the green reclining chair. One Hound obediently seats himself at the telephone table, while others, caught like boys at a game of musical chairs, stand helplessly, trying hard to look absolutely comfortable standing up. Ma has them bring in chairs from the porch and chairs from the dining room and the kitchen, even the chair down from Dad's room that he used to rest his slippers under when he went off to work.

And then here comes Herm from next door with a card table, followed by Emily trying to carry all four of its folding chairs at once.

Godfrey, Ma yells, forgetting herself, ready to go at it right there, what's the card table for?

She asked me for a card table, Ada, says Herm. Right behind Herm is his wife, Carol, carrying more chairs. Emily said you needed chairs, Ada.

Chairs, yes, says Ma, but not the whole ballroom at the Ritz. But the Hounds are eager to please and desperately eager to look settled, so they go to and set the card table up and the chairs around it and then they plunk their cans of beer on the table and sit down, just as if they'd been sitting there for years.

Ma insists that Herm and Carol sit down and that they have a can of beer too.

But . . . Godfrey! Wait a minute. Where in God's name are the chips and the cold cuts? Emily and Ma, followed by Artie Dove and Bill Cole, head back to the kitchen for the last of this evening's refreshments.

But . . . Lord almighty. With everyone spread out like this, where will they put the chips and the cold cuts so that everyone can get to them? People will have to keep standing up and sitting down. Ma is clearly panicked.

Oh come on, Ada, says Herm Krantz. These guys are grown men. Just put them on the card table and let them get something to eat when they're hungry.

But Ma will not hear of it. She sends Emily back to the kitchen for more bowls and trays. Emily is to bring them now and to meet Ma in the dining room where, from the sound of it, they are rearranging the chips and cold cuts to accommodate the clusters of men in every corner of the living room.

And then . . . at last, when Ma's hospitality has finally spun itself out and every Hound is where she thinks he ought to be, she settles down herself. But not without insisting that the men should be careful and not spill their beer.

On that note, the Hounds feel inspired to raise their cans of beer and take a sip.

Well, she adds, she doesn't have TV trays for everyone, but only for some.

And were these young men really old enough to drink beer?

And how could anyone stand to drink this stuff?

Right out of the can?

She didn't see how anyone could drink this stuff at all.

And what about you, Nate?

Don't tell me you're drinking?

Hey, I want a beer too, Ma, Emily croaks out. But Ma quells that rebellion with a fierce and terrible face.

For a dreadful long minute, everyone is quiet. But Tony Leonetti saves the day. Have you been to see your horse lately, Nate? he asks.

No, not lately, Tony.

Gee, Nate, I thought you couldn't go a day without seeing your horse, says Artie Dove, looking at the other Hounds for approval.

Well, Ma chimes in. If one of you can inspire him to go see his horse, I'll give you a million dollars. Jimmy—our son— came all the way over from Pennsylvania just to take him, but Nate backed out at the last minute. Now I keep telling him, Nate, you need to get up and out, but he won't listen.

Just likes to sit here all day. Either sits or sleeps. Today he slept half the day away.

A shade of color comes up in Dad's face. Hmmm, says Artie Dove. The Hounds are silent.

Well. Who takes care of your horse when you don't go, Nate? Chick Grote asks. He adjusts his glasses carefully over his nose.

We keep him at the polo club.

To the tune of two thousand dollars a year, says Ma. It didn't cost nearly that much to send the kids to college.

The Hounds are running out of things to ask and are afraid that anything more they say might set Ma off, but luckily our neighbor Herm from next door asks, When are you going to start singing? And then the evening begins in earnest.

The Hounds stayed past nine-thirty, though they hadn't planned to initially. Dad has really enjoyed himself, sitting on the green reclining chair, sipping on that can of beer that Ma has allowed him, listening to these men he has been a part of these last thirty years sing those songs that are so deep in his memory that he always wakes up in the morning hearing them. There were always snatches of them going on in his mind while he worked at the office or when he rode his horse or when he drove his car up to the stables.

> Last night I passed the corner
> Where we used to harmonize
> I didn't see a soul I used to know
> The neighborhood looked different . . .

He remembers how they sang that one in '75. A leaning in, brows dropped, on that first line, with a hand sweep to the right. Hand comes back on "harmonize," fists clenched and face squinting (dismay!) on "I didn't see a soul." Tenors and

baritones come on strong for the last line, then shoulders
slumped and oh so soft for the clincher:

> I began to realize
> How things can change in just a year or so . . .

Tony had them sing the program they had sung in '68
when the Hounds for Harmony were District Champions
and went on to compete in the Nationals. "Piano Roll Blues."
"Five Foot Two, Eyes of Blue." "Lida Rose." "Coney Island
Washboard." "At the Country Fair."

Ma insisted they do "Song and Dance Man" and Emily
wanted "My Wild Irish Rose," though when they sang it she
was surprised that it was so slow.

Has it always been like that? she wanted to know, her eyes
puzzled. Wasn't it ever real fast so you could clap your hands
to it?

Ma was fascinated by the fact that the Hounds had two new
members who were still boys, as she called them, though
they both were nearly twenty-two. She was even more astounded that they were able to drink beer. She remarked
on it more than once, every time, in fact, she offered them
another can of beer, which wasn't that often. But every can
of beer got drunk and all the trays of cold cuts and bowls
of chips and pretzels disappeared. And Emily even was able
to say a few things here and there, which the Hounds in
great consideration and politeness remarked on and laughed
cheerfully about. And Dad sang along in his fickle, off-key
voice on every number and grew more and more comfortable so that by the end of the evening, he was sad to see
his old friends depart. Though he was tired. Though they
insisted it was time for them to go, seeing him so worn, and
the next day being a work day for most of them.

Later—the dishes having been put in the dishwasher and

the garbage out, and the cans of beer collected on the back porch for Emily to take to the recycling center, and Emily actually asleep in her bed—Dad and Ma lay in their beds and talked.

It was very good of them to come over, Ma began.

Yes, Dad replied.

Although it wasn't exactly a surprise, what with them standing right on the corner where you could see them.

No, Dad agreed.

Didn't Artie Dove look good? And those two young boys? Drinking beer! Godfrey! Do you think they'll stay with the group?

We'll see . . .

And Emily really enjoyed herself.

She appeared to be content.

And what about you? Were you glad they came?

It was a very nice evening, Mother . . .

That was the summer.

November's come and with it the sharp, bright autumn weather Ma loves so well. Tomorrow is Thanksgiving. Dad's brother Lloyd is here from Kansas to spend the holiday. Emily will bring Fred to Thanksgiving dinner and Jimmy is coming over from Pennsylvania with his oldest boy, Phil.

But today the house is quiet. Ma is on the landing, looking out over the yard. She is brooding. It is an awkward time for hospitality. She wishes people would have stayed away and left them alone. They cannot pretend to anyone that Dad is doing well. They cannot pretend that Emily is normal. They cannot pretend that the house is set up for visitors.

Everything is out of kilter. Emily will not see a doctor. She refuses to take the pills that a previous doctor has prescribed. She has no work, nothing at all that occupies her. She spends most of the day on the couch in the living room.

If Fred calls her for a date, or if Ma asks her to do something for Dad, she swims up out of her stupor like someone who is close to drowning. When the call is over or the task accomplished, she returns to her post, sinks back into despair. Sleeps. Wakes from sleep to smoke cigarettes and stare at the walls or out the window at the roof next door.

And Ma is too worried about Dad to insist that Emily do something about herself or to do something for her or even to be able to think about what it is she should do.

And the cancer has advanced, grown bolder and bolder. Dad can hardly sleep, he aches so, but when Ma tries to rub his back or his legs, he cannot stand it. He cannot stand to be touched. Though he shivers, he cannot stand to have the blanket cover him, so sensitive have his bones become.

Each day brings new changes, new things to adjust to. It was barely a month ago that he had been able to get up and down the stairs. Then, as he grew weaker, they had set up quarters here on the landing. Here the sun comes in warmly in the morning. Dad could sit in a chair while Ma shaved him. She could bring him his breakfast and he could eat it off the little TV table she had Emily bring up from the living room. And when he got tired, he could manage the four stairs back up to his bed.

Then even that was too much. So they have begun to help him to Emily's room in the afternoons to get some sun while he sleeps in her bed.

He is asleep there now. There is no pretending anymore. Lloyd has come over thinking that he and Dad will spend their time reminiscing. But Dad cannot bear it, not even ten minutes of Lloyd's ruminations. Lloyd, of course, expects three meals a day, but that sort of domesticity has long ceased to exist. Dad does not come down for meals but eats what Ma can force down him when she brings his meals up to his bed. Ma, in fact, no longer cooks real meals but only whatever she can get Emily or Dad to eat, whenever they might decide to eat it.

Lloyd has many things to say to Ma about all this. He does not think that Emily is sick at all, not in the least, but simply stubborn. A recalcitrant girl. She needs work. She needs to be out on her own, living in her own place. Ma needs to stop treating her like a child.

He also thinks that Dad should make more of an effort to get up and around. Surely there is nothing so bad that it can't be helped by some exercise, by a little participation in life. Ma listens, not having the energy to explain the way she sees things, but she is glad when Lloyd says he thinks he'll walk downtown and do some Christmas shopping.

Emily has gone off with Fred to have some coffee. The house is quiet. The leafless trees in the back yard, the chill brisk air, the slight overcast call to Ma. She walks downstairs to the hall closet and puts on her coat, a scarf tucked around her neck, and sets out cautiously, grabbing hold of door and door frame, stoop and hedge as she goes down the front path, slowly, slowly, ever so slowly.

If her sight were good, like it used to be, she would move briskly, take a brisk invigorating walk, the kind of invigorating walk that both Emily and Dad should take every day. Well. No sense in pursuing that thought, but she does anyway, because Ma is a dreamer of dreams.

Oh, it matters not at all how far she gets today. Just the mailbox on the corner will be fine. It's not the walk so much but the air, just getting out of the house. The old sidewalk has erupted in spots, the roots of enormous trees pushing their way beneath it, summers and winters expanding and cooling it, and the broken spots and cracks are dangerous for her, so she puts each foot forward cautiously, tapping it on the sidewalk, stopping every so often to shut her eyes, lift her head, breathe deep, let the whole of her dreams distill in that sharp hopeful air.

She dreams. Dad is ambling down the back path, whistling, heading off to see his horse. She watches him from the back porch. He turns to wave to her and calls out, Come along with me, Mother. We can stop and have lunch together and talk and then you can read a book while I ride my horse. She watches Dad as he waits for her down near the rosebush beside the old garage. His face is flushed with color and he looks strong, so strong, and healthy.

Ma keeps walking, moving slowly toward the mailbox on the corner of the block. Now she is dreaming about Emily. Emily is out, striding around the block. She has just come home from work, a part-time clerical job she has in the morning where she gets paid well and is very much liked and appreciated by her employers. She's eaten a good lunch and wants to get in some exercise in the afternoon before she goes out to do her volunteer work at the hospital, before she heads out for dinner this evening with some of her girl-friends. Ma can see Emily as she walks, that same shiny black cap of hair she had when she was young, combed so neatly; she has on a crisp white blouse and a neatly ironed pair of slacks with a matching jacket. She waves and calls out, I'll be home in a half-hour, Ma.

Oh . . .

The thought of home makes Ma move a little quicker. She starts back toward the house. Maybe Dad's awake.

It is December and the house where I was born is full of shadows. It is the late afternoon. The pale light of winter retreats from the window of my father's bedroom. Ma has been up and down the stairs since early morning. She must insist that Dad eat, and if he refuses, that he at least take water. She must be there beside him to help him to the toilet or to change the pad beneath him if it gets soiled or to give him the medicine the doctor has prescribed.

Last week she wondered if they should take him down to the hospital, if they could do something for him there that she could not. But Dr. Skenk said that there was nothing at all that they could do for him and that if Ma could tend to him, he would be better off there with her and with Emily.

Emily has spent her waking hours downstairs on the living room couch, smoking and dreaming. Ma has told her not to make any plans at all today. She must be ready to come up and take her place beside Dad in case Ma has to go down and fix some food or go to the bathroom. It might even be necessary for her to run to the store for Ma, but if she does, she must come right back and not stall around at Grunings.

Emily!

It is Emily's appointed hour. Dad has indicated that he needs to get up on his toilet chair but Ma feels unable to lift him herself, for fear she might drop him. Emily is to get hold of him on the one side while Ma takes the other. Together they get him settled and it is just as Ma expected. He didn't really have to go, he just felt that pressure on his bladder like he'd been feeling it all these last months.

Are you done, Nate? He doesn't answer, but she is used to that. He has stopped talking altogether in the past few days. So she fusses at Emily instead, cautioning her. But oh, he's so heavy!

Be careful, Emily! she says sharply. Don't drop him!

But Emily knows instinctively that it doesn't matter anymore. He's dead, she says in a flat voice.

And it's true. They lay him back down and there is no life in him anywhere, not in his heart, or in his face, or in his breath. Ma is stunned and falls on him, crying out that she is sorry, she is so sorry. Oh, she is so sorry.

Emily is watching Ma. She is frightened to hear her so, her voice so full of remorse. She will describe it to us later when we come back home for the funeral.

Dad died in my arms, she will tell us. And you should have seen Ma when she realized he was dead! She was crying and saying over and over again that she was sorry. Oh, I'm so sorry, Nate, she kept saying.

Ma will deny that she said any such thing. Emily, she will say sharply, you're just making it up.

But right now, right now, with Dad there, without his life in him, lying in this bed he lay in for so long, she is sorry, she is so sorry.

She puts it away though, for years to come, when she herself is getting sick and the days and the nights are so very long and she is weary. She will talk to him then in her mind the way she wanted to talk to him while he lived. Complaining at first about all the usual things. The horse. The polo club. The two houses at the shore that he should have bought. But then, full of sorrow and confessing to him all those things that she felt she should have been for him and was completely unable to be.

The ambulance is called. And behind them come the men from Ford's funeral home. They want a suit and a shirt and a tie that they can dress him in to be buried. She must rummage through his closet to find something. He hasn't worn anything but pajamas and his robe for months. Everything is dusty. They want her to sign papers and seem determined to hurry and get him out of the house.

Are you sure he's dead? she keeps asking them, one after the other. The ambulance driver. The lady with him who is a paramedic. The men from the funeral home.

You're going to take him now? she asks after she has settled it that he is dead. It all seems so hasty, so hastily done, such an abrupt and final break in the vital routine they had established.

But they have him ready. They have his suit and his shirt and his tie. They have the papers all signed. They put him on a stretcher and cover him over with a sheet. And then they set out.

Ma and Emily watch as they carry Dad down the stairs, down to the landing. From the windows they can see the funeral home van, waiting with its back door open there on the macadam court. They take him down to the first floor, through the kitchen, down the back steps, down the back path. They put his body in the van and shut the door and then he is gone.

Ma stands on the top step of the porch and watches them pull away. She scratches her head and studies the porch floor for a long time. Sighs. It is the way he always did things. Just going down the back path without so much as saying goodbye.

She goes inside to call us.

He's gone, she says. Your father is dead.

She's alone there in the house that night. Fred has called Emily and wants a date. Emily stands waiting beside the phone, wanting to know if it's all right. Dad won't mind, will he? she asks Ma.

Ma thinks to complain and tell her that it's not appropriate to go out on a date on the very day your father dies. But Emily has so few pleasures, Ma hates to deny her even one of them. Who will notice? Or care?

Go ahead, she tells her. Just go on.

Plans for a Wedding

Emily Field, wrenched between the overwhelming desire to have—JUST ONE!—another cigarette and the equally overwhelming desire, at last, to vindicate—NO!—finally, once and for all, *justify* herself in the eyes of those thousands—the old neighbors surrounding her at 4401 Polk, her sister and her brother, the girls in the office pool at Marquardt & Smith, her mother—MAAAAAAA— and her father, and that long line of trash who had said, declared it in the hallways of Richman High, that she was stupid—Hey, you, you soooooo stupid!—who had so tenaciously watched her progress ever since when? she could not, would not ever be able to, remember . . . pulled a soggy cardboard box down from the shelf in her closet and began throwing its contents out on top of her bed, listening, but only partially, NOT with her complete attention—I can hear you, but I am definitely not listening!—to the insistent voices of a legion who were most assuredly talking about her. Her hand flew to the top of her head, pressing in there, around and around, as she strained to avoid them, yet to hear. Was it about her? Did they say Poor Emily?

Hurry it up, would you? It's nearly six o'clock.

Six! The night had begun. November and snow. Dark already, long dark, the night dark and pressing its weight—she could feel it—against the old trailer. And the moon. Looking in at the bedroom window. She slammed the curtains together fast. Hurry! Hurry! Get out of here!

Jennifer and Bernie, who had sensed and seen her excitement ever since she came in the door, yipped and yapped and jumped up and down on the bed, barking for her to bring her face down so they could lick it all over.

Which she did, which she always did for her little children who loved her and did not ever criticize, even when she might leave them alone in the trailer maybe all day or overnight. But there were times she could not stay here, days and nights she could not stay here, whole days and nights she just had to spend out, sitting in the Dunkin Donuts shop on East Third Street or, if that failed, if she wore out her welcome, and she knew full well when she had worn out her welcome, the girl Trish speaking to her so rudely—isn't it about time, Emily? isn't it just about time?—going to the all-night coffee place at the crossroads, just for a few more cups of coffee, just a few, because she was rattled and she needed to sit and think. And finally, if the waitresses questioned her or if they complained to the manager and got him to ask her to move on, coming home, but slowly, down that long dark road, when all else failed, to this . . . box.

No! NO! She hadn't said that. HER home. She loved it.

Ma. I love my home, I take good care of it. I mow the lawn. I do mow the lawn. I'll never live anywhere else! I like living out of town like this, down the long country road, even in the dark. Only . . .

Jennifer and Bernie never criticized her. They were her

little children. But not for long. For there would soon be other children. Make room, Jennifer and Bernie. Make way, dogs. Very soon, there would be real children and she would have many children, just like her sister Adele had. Children and a husband and a home of her own. The yard would be full of children and there would be children at her table and she would cook for them and her husband would be out in the yard tossing a football back and forth to the children before dinner. Just like Adele's husband, Bernie. Adele had a husband and so would she.

And yet—she did not know what she would do if the dogs ran out on the road and got killed.

She sank down on the edge of the bed. She would die.

She would wear black to their funeral. She had seen funerals at the pet cemetery up the road. Black dress, black gloves, black veil. All the people in the trailer park would come. We know what a good owner you've been. What a shame this has happened.

Or would they say instead, stand there and say, their fingers poking away at her face, this is what happens when you won't keep your dogs on a chain? Like we told you a thousand times.

Step on it! He'll be calling you any minute. Look, it's nearly six-fifteen and you haven't bathed and do you have clean clothes and what about your underwear and what about . . .

Hurry! Hurry!

No. Here is the way it would be. No one would ever criticize her again. Not when they saw these letters she was looking for, the ones that ought to have been in the box in her closet. No one would ever criticize her again, not when they understood who the letters were going to be taken to. Not when they saw Emily at her own wedding because of this, this one thing in a long series of things that would get her to the church, down the aisle, to the reception.

Oh, the reception. Hundreds of people. Hundreds of new faces. All of Arnie's relatives. Herself in white—white? it would have to be white now—the center of attention, the center of thousands of new faces.

And they wouldn't be criticizing her. Not the bride. Though Ma would. Ma criticized every bride she'd ever seen—their dresses, their hair, the alcohol on their father's breath, the invited guests, the too long and weary preaching of the ministers, the godawful, GODAWFUL!, reception afterward. And never enough food. Or too much, a terrible waste of money.

Every bride but Roxanne Tice. Roxanne Tice's wedding was perfect. Because her mother—Marie Tice—had made it so. But Marie Tice made all things perfect. Her husband Al's too-small income, the darling clothes of her darling children, the upholstery of every chair in her house, the meals she cooked, the dresses she wore. There was no keeping up with Marie Tice and no bride but Roxanne that had ever satisfied Ma!

Emily threw first one envelope and then another out of the box and onto the bed. She had packed the box last year, when she had finally packed up and moved out and used what Fred Monroe had left her to buy this trailer and gotten up and away from her mother, which, finally, was what she should have done years before, way back even in the beginning—Yes Yes—way back in the beginning. Even if she was only thirteen. The inexplicable twisting in her head. The terror of things. The absolute fear. She should just have moved out. Just moved out. Oh yes. Arnie had said so. And Arnie knew best. She had talked to him a long time about it this afternoon, first at the Dunkin Donuts and then in her car. He had said so about her, had said so about himself. The best thing in the world, Emily, is to move out and away from one's mother at any cost.

Because you see what has happened to me, he told her. It's going to be hard for her to let me go now if I want to get married.

Oh, but his mother would have to let him go. The letters, the icing on the cake, the passport out of darkness. Wait until Arnie's mother saw the letters!

Because he had also said he thought he'd ask his mother if Emily could come over for dinner tonight.

Emily had stuffed the box full of big manila envelopes crammed tight with miscellaneous papers. Clippings from the newspaper. Old bank statements. Dust flew up and made her cough violently and frightened Jennifer and Bernie, who had been shooed off the bed because of their disruptive behavior—they made it hard for her to think, scurrying underfoot, nearly as anxious as she—and some dust that must have been left over from her mother's house settled on the yellowed chenille bedspread.

The letters she was looking for, the letters she had written to the editor of the *Dispatch*, had to be in here somewhere.

Of course I kept at least one copy!

Don't tell me I've given them all away, she said out loud, panicked suddenly lest Ma find out she had done something so thoughtless.

Hurry!

Her letters to the editor just weren't there!

But she had to have the letters to show Arnie's mother tonight at dinner. They had been accepted for publication, not one letter, but two, and one right after the other.

One right after the other.

She would show her the letters and then she would tell her a little about her plans to write more letters and to become an author like her sister Adele.

She would tell Mrs. Detwiler her plans for another letter; this one was going to be about the men that she had picked up outside of MacDonald's. Decent hardworking men. A preacher and a man in construction who had been traveling all over Florida and Pennsylvania and whose car had broken down and who had run out of money, and how she took them home to live with her for a week until they could get some money and she had shared all her meals with them and how she had told them, Listen fellas, no monkey business. Hands off! You can stay here, but hands off, and how she had gone over to Ma's and borrowed a little food from Ma and then . . .

And then. When supper was over and Emily had told Mrs. Detwiler all about herself and when Arnie had said how deeply in love he was with Emily, Emily would tell Mrs. Detwiler all about the plans she had for the wedding.

But how could she without the letters!

You don't have a stitch of clean underwear. And would you look at the clock? Would you? Just look at the clock?

It was a quarter to seven. She ran out of the bedroom, with the box turned out every which way on her bed, slammed the door behind her and headed down the tight dark hallway of her trailer. Jennifer and Bernie scurried along at her heels, vying for first place behind her, yapping and nipping at each other as they went.

The letters were such wonderful letters. They weren't like any other letters anyone had ever seen. They didn't criticize. I'm not that sort of girl, Emily said out loud.

No, these letters were thank-yous, broad open thank-yous. They told people thank you for the good that they had done. And they were—at least the ones planned for the future— about good deeds, kindness. There were some opinions, but there was definitely no politics. And only an opinion or two. But how could a person help having an opinion about the good senator who had taken a gun to his mouth and shot himself in front of the TV cameras? Did the American public or press know that in the human mind there are valves that stop a person from thinking, from talking, stop one from smiling, that just shut down and cannot for the life of one be brought up again? Did the American public know or recognize that this man was emotionally troubled and could not help himself? Did they understand how pitiable is the condition of a mind that cannot think? Could they forgive him like they had DeLorean who lost his wife and dyed his hair and went around with a colored woman and even went to jail, who then wrote a book, and then was acquitted? Could they be so lenient? This senator should have been encouraged to join social clubs and the people around him should have been kinder and liked him better. A man's ego is such a terrible thing to hurt.

Yes, in this matter of the senator, Emily Minton Field did have an opinion. And she was willing to share it. And she knew that people would appreciate her for it.

You don't often find people like me, Emily said. She opened the cupboard in the kitchen. On one of the dusty almost empty shelves, between a couple of cans of tomato soup and a box of Lipton instant chicken noodle soup—that soup had NOT been there for ages, as certain people might want to say, she had just recently purchased those cans and she had been eating well, nobody's business but her own—was another worn-looking manila envelope which she pulled out quickly. She turned it upside down onto the kitchen counter.

There! She HAD made many copies of both letters and here they were.

If you're late, they'll never ask you back.

I really thought ahead, didn't I? she said and this time she was addressing her mother, Ma, who sat across town, most likely in her chair in the living room watching the news, and who did not believe that Emily ever thought ahead or ever thought, as a matter of fact, of anything but herself.

Emily studied the opening paragraphs of each letter. Arnie's mother would be glad to see that her son had fallen so deeply in love with a decent girl, one who didn't criticize or complain or go around sleeping with men.

Now, this first letter was her best. This letter about Jennifer and Bernie would be sure to claim Mrs. Detwiler's heart.

Emily pulled shut the drapes in the living room and sat down on the couch and Jennifer and Bernie jumped up beside her and on her lap and licked her face and her lips and she puckered them together so they could have their fill of kisses and then pushed them aside. Be quiet, now, children, she said, making them sit quietly while she read her first ever accepted letter to the editor out loud:

"There are times in this life of ours when things work just right and now is one of those times. What was plus on my side was that I have a good home life and I am able to give someone a good life and comfort them. What was plus on Jennifer and Bernie's side was that they had no home but were very cute. And did you guess it? Jennifer and Bernie are dogs and I found them at the SPCA.

"Jennifer and Bernie are my whole life. I wouldn't think of spending my time without them. I'm not like some who for example go out after work and stop to have a drink or two or never come home at the risk of breaking family ties. Jennifer and Bernie are always my first thought and whether I come or I go, they are always by my side.

"I take them to the mall all dressed up in their winter coats. Not a day goes by that someone doesn't ask, 'Where did you get such cute little dogs?' It is then that I tell them about our own SPCA. 'Go there,' I say. 'You will find a dog who can really love and appreciate you just for who you are.'

"Jennifer and Bernie are not just nice. They are good dogs and always obey me. I am not like some who will let their animals go undisciplined. Jennifer and Bernie are completely well-behaved. If you want joy in your heart, go to our very own SPCA and find your own dogs and then be like me and spread the word all over town."

Signed, Emily Field, Emily read. She had just begun reading the second letter—"THE TRUE MEANING OF THE WORD LOVE"—when the phone rang.

It was her mother.

What are you doing? she asked Emily.

Nothing, said Emily quickly.

I want you to come over and help me clean out the closet in my bedroom.

Oh, I can't do that, said Emily, but she did not immediately have an excuse at hand. What she couldn't say, what she couldn't talk about, what she couldn't tell Ma was that Mrs. Detwiler had invited her for dinner. Ma would start telling her everything, over and over again, and of course, she wouldn't see, she would never understand. Her mother had already insisted that Emily not ever mention Arnie's name to her again. Ever. And that was only because Emily had told her mother one night two weeks ago that she and Arnie had gone out on their first date. But that they had known each other for a long time, more than two weeks—why had Ma kept insisting it was only two weeks?—it was much more than two weeks. A month, at least. Maybe six.

And that they were in love.

Actually, she had told her mother that they were deeply in love.

Actually, she had told her mother that they were deeply in love and had decided to get married and have four kids.

Don't ever talk to me about it again, Mrs. Field had said and buried her white head and long nose into her hands and refused to talk to Emily anymore and wouldn't look up until Emily had left.

Her sister Adele had four kids. Her brother Jimmy had two kids. They were both married. Other people were deeply in love. Why not her?

I'm a grown woman, Ma! Emily yelled into the telephone.

Yeah, said her mother. What's being a grown woman have to do with coming over and helping me clean my closet?

I don't always have to say why I can't go, do I? Emily yelled again.

Don't yell into the telephone, Emily. And you're not going out with that boy again, are you? Mrs. Field demanded.

He's not a boy, Ma. He's thirty-seven.

You told me last week that he was thirty-eight.

Thirty-seven. Almost thirty-eight, said Emily. His mother, A LOVELY WOMAN, has invited me to come to dinner, she spit out.

When did you meet his mother?

I've met his mother.

When?

She told Arnie that she wanted to get to know me.

Does she know you?

Arnie is deeply in love with me, Ma!

Don't yell into the phone, said Mrs. Field. And you listen to me: you are forty-five years old. This man is probably not even thirty. And he's blind. And he's crippled. Whether his mother is lovely or not.

Blindness is minor to me, Ma, said Emily. I don't judge a book by its cover. Arnie is a very beautiful man and he's very religious. He goes to church every Sunday and twice during the middle of the week. And he's deeply in love with me and wants me for life.

Oh, go on, said Mrs. Field. I can't stand to talk to you. And she hung up.

Emily went thrashing through the trailer again, looking for the typewriter that might work, whose ribbon might still have some ink on it. And found it, after some little exercise, behind the couch, and smelling like the dogs had peed on it. But she brought it out and wiped the cover off with the dishrag; she opened the case up and sat down.

The phone rang. It was her mother again.

What do you mean, she invited you for dinner? Do you know it's nearly seven? What time did she invite you for dinner?

Yeah, said Emily.

Yeah, what?

Yeah, around eight. Arnie says they eat around eight.

Do you have any clean clothes? You haven't done any wash in a week. You should have left by now. She lives all the way into town and that will take you at least a half-hour. Did you take a bath? Where does she live?

Arnie's going to call me and give me directions.

When?

Soon. Get off the phone.

Emily hung up.

Pulling a piece of lined paper out of an old notebook, she began a letter to her sister Adele.

Adele:

I have good news for you. I have been seeing a wonderful man by the name of Arnie for quite some time.

Arnie is a warm and wonderful man with a wonderful sense of humor and he is very religious. He's 35 years old, but age means nothing to me.

We are planning to be married in September of this year. We are deeply in love and want each other for life. Arnie is planning to buy me a ring. He is the president of his own company.

I want you to come to the wedding. I will send you the money for your flight, unless we run out of money. Then Ma can pay for you to come.

We want just a small and simple wedding, no more than 200 people with 100 relatives coming to the reception.

I'm not depending on Ma financially anymore as Arnie, as I mentioned priorly, is the president of his own company and is a manager and a consultant. He is in the home products line and is taking a class at school in computers to boost him up in his sales. We are completely financially independent.

Ma is not coming to my wedding as we are fighting. She says that Arnie will be a burden to me and that she will end up supporting both of us, but this is not true.

Let me talk to you heart-to-heart. Arnie can feed himself and dress himself, shower, take care of his own needs, even shave. Blindness is a minor problem to me. I want a sunshiny personality with no drinking or running around. Arnie is perfect to me in my eyes.

If you want to call and congratulate me, do so.

Your sister, Emily

P.S. No bad remarks.

Jennifer and Bernie frisked around at the legs of her kitchen chair.

Emily turned the TV on and sat down in front of it. She lit a cigarette, studying the TV screen intensely, and began to make her plans.

At the wedding, there would be five bridesmaids. Adele could be one of them. Her brother's wife could be another, but only if she didn't criticize. That made two.

Are you watching the clock? Do you see what time it is?

Tonight she would find out if Arnie had any sisters. If he

did, they could use one or two of them, depending on what they were like and whether they agreed that this wedding was a good thing.

If he didn't have any sisters, she would consider asking Helen who sold donuts at the Dunkin Donut shop on the night shift if she would be a bridesmaid and she was sure that Helen would say yes. Though that would make Trish, who was the other girl that worked the shift with Helen, mad, but she couldn't possibly ask Trish because Trish had snickered when she told her last week that she was deeply in love, and then said, You mean, with that blind guy that hitchhikes all over town? The one who's crippled?

When she and Mrs. Detwiler talked over the plans this evening, Emily would mention that she would wear a pale pastel blue dress, because this was a winter wedding and because she had been married before. And she would wear a pale pastel blue dress, even though, well, even though she had already put down fifteen dollars, well, okay, a hundred dollars, on a white dress.

I was just passing the store on the way down the road to home!

It had a long train. And a veil. Because really she was a virgin, if you wanted to get into technicalities. If anyone cared to ask. Because Fred Monroe had, well, it wasn't the sort of thing you talked about at a wedding. Suffice it to say that Fred took care of himself and she herself wasn't interested in that sort of thing. And let that be all she would say about the matter of marriage with Fred Monroe. He was dead anyway.

Of course, marriage with Arnie would be different, considering the four kids they wanted and all. And that was why she would really end up wearing the white dress. Without any explanation whatsoever. That was just the way it would be. Let people say what they might.

Five bridesmaids. There would be then five groomsmen

and Arnie would wear a pale blue suit to offset and complement her dress, which would work even if at the last minute
she got afraid to wear the white dress with the long train
and actually she didn't really see how she could back out on
that deal, she had already put her money down on that dress
and she didn't have a pale blue dress anyway and she herself
would lead him up the aisle so he wouldn't fall or bump
into the pews. It would be different than most weddings.
Highly unusual. But, under the circumstances, all of Arnie's
relatives and friends would understand how deeply he and
Emily were in love. And because her own father wasn't alive,
it was entirely appropriate that the man she was going to live
with for the rest of her life would walk with her up the aisle.

The phone rang. It was her mother again.

Godfrey! You haven't left yet?

I'm waiting for Arnie to call.

What time's he supposed to call?

Around seven.

Emily! It's seven-thirty.

He'll call. Don't bug me, Ma.

You are not to go to that woman's house and bedevil her
with your ridiculous plans, her mother said.

We are deeply in love, Ma. Nothing you can do or say can
take away the love we feel for each other.

Oh stop. You wouldn't know love if it hit you like a ton
of bricks. And there's plenty I can do and plenty I can say
that will make it impossible for you to even consider getting
married. Plenty.

No, Ma, this is true love. Arnie and I want each other for
life and want to have a family together . . .

You are too old to have children. And this man is a cripple.

He's not a cripple, Ma! And he's not too old. He's thirty-
two!

Godfrey! Thirty-two! The last time I talked to you he was thirty-eight.

Emily couldn't think of anything to say.

And I've talked to Rose next door. You're just dreaming again, just like you did with Fred. Rose says she knows who Arnie is, she's seen him hitchhiking around town for years. Do you know how come he's blind?

Huh?

She told me that he was robbing a house when he was fifteen and the owner shot him so badly that he lost his sight and he barely has any function in his hands. And he is not the president of some company. He sells Amway and his parents support him completely. He lives at home with his parents.

They love him! They want him to live at home!

For godsakes, what's a thirty-two-year-old man doing living at home with his parents unless they're supporting him?

Thirty-eight. He's thirty-eight, going on thirty-nine.

Thirty-two! You just don't think. You have no way to support yourself. You haven't been able to hold a job in the last ten years for more than a month. And he can't support himself. You know who will end up supporting the two of you?

We will.

No, I will.

Well, you can help us if you want.

And he has no idea what you're like.

That's not true, Ma. He knows all about me. I told him everything.

About the breakdowns?

Yeah. Yeah.

The hospitals?

Yeah, Ma.

Those last few months with Fred?

Huh?

And what about when you tried to kill yourself? Did you tell him about that?

Yeah. Yeah. We tell each other everything.

Did you know he was blind because he got shot?

Yeah. Hey, Ma, I've been thinking about the wedding. Arnie and I want to invite all our friends and relatives. But it will be small. Just a hundred people or so.

Oh, Emily, you're not going to tell his mother that, are you? She'll think you're completely crazy.

Arnie's already told her all about me and I'm bringing her the newspaper articles I've had published. In fact, I'm going to write another one right now.

Emily. Emily. Emily could hear her mother groaning and knew she had her eyes covered and was shaking her head back and forth. I hope she tells you to leave him alone. I don't want to hear another thing about him. And don't you ever dare to bring him over here. I don't want the neighbors to see him.

She hung up.

Jennifer wanted outside, but it was already too late for Bernie. He had made a mess over in the corner. When Emily went to clean it up, she found more behind the chair, which she scooped up hastily, because already a letter was forming itself in her head. She sat back down to the typewriter.

To the Editor: Love is a thing of beauty, found like a beautiful flower in the midst of weeds. The world is full of weeds, but love will suddenly sprout up when you aren't expecting it. The world will try its best to trample the lovely flower underfoot, but true love can't be . . .

Emily squeezed her face together. But true love can't be— Cut down? Hurt? Mowed under?

She rocked back and forth in her chair. This was the truth,

finally, it was really the truth. Something blossoming, about to sprout, something lovely, and the world, in the guise of her mother, no less, was going to smash . . . Her yard outside was green, full of grass, even though it was winter. She pictured it in her mind's eye. She pictured herself last summer mowing it. She mowed it. She mowed it all right. Once a week, sooner if need be. But the landlady. Calling Ma. Love mowed down, like that, tall high grass just cropped short and How come you didn't mow it once a week? It's an eyesore, that's what it is, Emily. Your yard is an eyesore. And those filthy dogs. If you let those dogs run loose just one more time . . .

True love turned under, wildflowers of love turned under and . . .

She needed another cigarette. Eight o'clock. Maybe the deal was that she was supposed to go to Arnie's house at seven. Wasn't he going to call and give her directions? Right. That had to be it. Because she couldn't have come to eat supper without directions anyway. Though she could have looked him up in the phone book. Maybe that was what she should do.

Maybe he had tried to call when Ma was on the phone. Ma had stayed on the phone a long time. But maybe he said for her to come to the Dunkin Donuts at seven. Maybe that's what he said.

She dialed Dunkin Donuts. Yeah, hi. Hi. Who's this? Helen? Trish? It's me, Emily. Let me speak to Arnie, will you?

And then, of course, she had to explain to Trish all about the wedding and even, in fact, felt like she had to ask her to be a bridesmaid, but would later tell her no, because all Trish said was, Sure, Emily. I'll believe it when I see it. And she didn't want anyone at the wedding who was going to criticize.

But Arnie wasn't there, hadn't been there all night or any

time during the day after he'd been there with Emily. Emily hung up.

She sat down. And just for a second realized that what he had said, in fact, was that his mother would never let him marry, it didn't matter much if he was in love. Though he did agree with Emily that he loved her. He wanted her to come meet his mother someday.

She lit another cigarette. The phone rang.

Just exactly what did he say? Emily's mother asked. Was he going to call at seven or eat at seven? I think he's left you in the lurch.

No, said Emily. He didn't leave me. He loves me. He tried to call me when you were on the phone and he couldn't get through.

How do you know that?

That's what happened.

Well, now what are you going to do?

I'll just drive over to his house.

Where does he live?

It's in the phone book.

You can't do that.

Look, Ma said after a long silence, I need some help with my closet. Her voice suddenly got tender. Why don't you come over here and I'll fix you a nice supper.

Emily didn't answer.

Emily?

She was thinking about Trish who had criticized her and how surprised that Trish would be when Emily was actually married and immediately she pictured her four kids and Arnie around a summer picnic table in the yard with the grass trim and tidy and then she started thinking about the dress she had the hundred dollars down on and how she'd have to see if Ma would give her the rest of the money. And then too of the night, how much of it lay ahead of her.

You can spend the night here, her mother said.

Yeah, okay, Emily rasped finally into the phone and hung up. And then nothing much mattered after that, not the TV being on, not the dogs barking, not the door and the necessity of locking it, not her purse that lay open on the couch. But only just getting up and getting out, quickly, pushing out down the long road before the night pressed itself in any closer against her.

JAMES DEAN

About the Author

Lee Merrill Byrd grew up in New
Jersey but has spent the past twenty
years in the Southwest, mainly in
Texas. With her husband, poet
Bobby Byrd, she established Cinco
Puntos Press, a regional press focusing
on the literature of the American
West. They have a daughter and two
sons and live in El Paso.